Balboa Shores

by Peggy Penwell Marsh

"Life isn't about waiting for the storm to pass. It's about learning to dance in the rain."

In memory of my mother, Mildred Irene Owen Penwell Ineich, who danced in the rain with sparkle and shine.

ACKNOWLEDGEMENTS

I would like to thank the Sacramento State University Renaissance Society's Writers Group One, both current members as well as those no longer with us, who for so long gave me their time, knowledge, patience and support. I will always be grateful.

I would also like to thank my wonderfully talented daughter, Susan Marsh, who edited this manuscript and guided it toward publication.

Last, but very importantly, thanks go to photographer Tim Carmichael for the cover art. Tim is proprietor of Thee Hubbell House Bed & Breakfast at 307 West Elm Street in Winnsboro, TX. www.theehubbellhouse.com

CHAPTER 1
AUGUST

Driving up to Balboa Shores Assisted Living Facility for Memory-Impaired Seniors, head caregiver Patsy Smith felt as if she were coming home. Home to a grand plantation house with white portico, a lush veranda and heavy beveled glass doors. The front patio was lined with a variety of potted fern, hosta, and cyclamen. Iron benches were set around the entrance, where seniors and their visitors could sit and enjoy the sweet scent of jasmine wafting from the trellises.

Patsy parked her car in the spot assigned for staff and was practically bouncing as she came through the front doors. After stashing her purse in her office, she proceeded toward apartment 241. As she approached, she heard a muffled, frantic voice. Entering the spacious apartment filled with sunlight from the large lace-covered windows, Patsy encountered Miss Millie, sitting daintily on her flowered chintz sofa.

Miss Millie was leaning over and shouting into the telephone. "I swallowed my battery! Is it poison? Am I going to die?" Raising her head, she spotted Patsy and immediately hung up the phone. "Oh Patsy, my angel, thank goodness you're here," said Miss Millie, fluttering her hands. Patsy *did* look

1

somewhat angelic, with her wheat-colored hair pulled back into a high ponytail and loose tendrils curling like a halo around her sun-kissed face. "I swallowed a battery to my hearing aid, and I'm scared it's going to kill me."

Seating herself next to Miss Millie, Patsy put an arm around her. "Tell me how in the world did you swallow it? Are you sure?"

"I did, I did, I swallowed it! I got up early this morning like I always do, and was sitting on the couch reading the newspaper. I was still in my nightgown. You know, the one with the pink roses and my pink robe with the fluffy feather collar and those wonderful matching slippers."

"Yes, yes, I know them well," said Patsy. "Tell me what happened with your hearing aid battery."

"That's what I'm telling you. One of the caregivers came to give me my pills. I think it was that new one Julie ... or Julia...or maybe it's Judy?"

"And...?" Patsy coaxed, her hands trying to pull the information from Miss Millie.

"I took the pills, like a good girl, and went on reading my paper. After Julia left, I saw something on the floor. I thought maybe I'd dropped one of my pills so I picked it up, popped it in my mouth, and swallowed it. When Judy came back to help me dress and put in my hearing aids, she said one of the batteries was missing. Well, it must have been on the floor and I mistook it for a pill and swallowed it." Miss Millie put her hands in her soft white hair and shook her head, loosening the curls in the carefully coiffed up-do. "Oh my god, Patsy, do you think it will kill me?"

"I don't believe so, Miss Millie. It'll probably go right through you, but I'll check with the nurse just to make sure. Is that who you were talking to when I came in?"

"No, I was so upset I called my daughter in Portland."

Patsy smiled. "In Portland? What could she possibly do about it so far away?"

"I don't know, Patsy, I just didn't know what else to do. My daughter's much better in a crisis than I am."

"I think you'll be okay, and we probably won't need to do anything except maybe order some more batteries."

"No no, I have plenty ... as long as I don't keep eating them. The girls put in a new one and I'm all set for the day."

"Good, then let's just take your sugar count and you can go down to breakfast." Patsy stuck Miss Millie's finger, squeezed the tip to raise a drop of blood, and took the count. "133, Miss Millie," said

Patsy as she recorded the number. "You're good to go."

Miss Millie smiled, got up, and started toward the door. "Wait, Miss Millie," Patsy called. "I think we might want to comb your hair just a bit before you go downstairs, and don't forget to use your walker. We don't want any falls."

Miss Millie turned to face Patsy. "Walker? Walker schmalker," she protested. "I shouldn't need a walker just to go downstairs to breakfast."

"Shouldn't doesn't have anything to do with it. *Must* is the word Dr. Neil used."

After seeing Miss Millie safely on her way to breakfast, Patsy made her way through the foyer to the Activities Room to put chairs in a circle for Memory Games. She smiled as she passed residents, taking in their shared features – white hair, walkers, slow gaits. The residents were family to her, each one so dear and unique. Her eyes made her way around the room and rested on Catherine.

Okay, maybe not *everyone* was dear, but Catherine was certainly unique.

Catherine Kingston Hughes, decked out in a long flowing skirt and tall black boots, was sitting in the overstuffed chair close to the front entrance. Her long gray hair was tucked under a colorful bandana and topped with a black gaucho hat. A large oil portrait and a small cloth satchel sat on the floor beside her. Although Catherine preferred to dress like an aging hippie, she was tall and exuded a steadfast and aristocratic presence. It was no surprise that she was quickly but affectionately labeled *Catherine the Great* by the staff at Balboa Shores.

"Good morning, Catherine," said Patsy. Catherine raised an eyebrow but did not respond. *Why hasn't anyone done something about Catherine sitting by the front door again? Surely someone besides me could help her back to her room.* Glancing through the blinds covering the window of a large office, she saw Susan Jackson, Balboa Shores' executive director and Patsy's boss. *On the phone, as usual. Why hasn't she dealt with Catherine? Couldn't she handle these sorts of problems once in a while?*

Patsy continued to the Activities Room thinking *I'll deal with Catherine later.*

CHAPTER 2

The large open Activities Room could be closed off, making two separate areas, each with its own entrance. One side had rows of padded folding chairs set up for large group presentations, the other had tables for playing games, crafts, puzzles, and such. Light spilled into the pale, sage green room from the wall of windows that framed a beautiful Japanese maple tree just beginning to change color. The contrast in colors caught Patsy's eye and she felt a pang of sadness, remember how much Bud had loved fall.

Beyond the maple tree, a healing garden beckoned those seeking peace within its verdant greenery and the sound of trickling water. Inside, in front of the windows, sat couches and comfortable leather chairs along with a large screen TV. The chirping sound of Clementine, the resident canary, and the smell of popcorn gave the room a homey feel.

After she set up the last chair, residents began to wander in from breakfast and take their seats. In the circle sat Olga, a Swede with a thick accent, red lipstick, and heavy lens glasses that enlarged her eyes, giving her an owlish look. Her fair hair and skin made her appear younger than Patsy knew her to be. Olga was a dyed-in-the-wool Republican. Her husband had worked in the Eisenhower administration and she wore her elephant brooch, necklace, and bracelet proudly every day. She would make no compromise in a discussion, political or not.

Miss Millie, a vivacious cross between Miss Marple and Eva Gabor, sat next to Olga. Anytime Olga tried to engage her in a serious debate, Miss Millie just laughed and changed the subject. She didn't know – or want to know – a thing about politics. She might wear an Uncle Sam hat on the Fourth of July, but that was because she was into having fun and dressing up for all occasions. She even owned a dress covered with shamrocks for St. Patrick's Day and a variety of holiday wear: antlers, Santa hats, bunny ears, headbands with bats, hearts, and even one with sparklers that she wore on New Years Eve and the Fourth of July.

Next sat Beatrice. Beatrice had a tendency to "find" things, things that didn't always belong to her. Beatrice was a first-class wanderer, which made it challenging to find her when she wasn't where she was supposed to be. Beatrice would often wander off into other residents' rooms, just walk in and sit down as if she were right at home.

Maisie, who had been a professional dancer, wore a pair of her sparkling red dance shoes as she sat next to Beatrice. Maisie was slight and lithe, with delicate features, and with her soft, fine hair she looked as if she could be a fairy if you just added some wings and handed her a wand. She had a virtual rainbow of dancing shoes stored in her room.

Sarah, the oldest resident, was a spinster who had spent most of her life as a missionary in India. She was frail, shy, and soft-spoken. If Maisie was a fairy, then Sarah was more of an angel.

Flirty Alletta sat between Sarah and Harry. Alletta dyed her hair a light auburn and kept up with the latest fashions. Her makeup was always done before she left her room. Her diamond rings, tennis bracelet, and earrings let everyone know she came from money − mostly by way of her four ex-husbands.

Harry Howell, the newest resident of Balboa Shores and a self-proclaimed ladies man, was tall and distinguished-looking, with plenty of wavy white hair, bright blue eyes, and a sparkling smile. Singing was Harry's passion, but his business had been construction. He started his company, Howell and Son, in 1936. Now it was run by his oldest son, Casey.

In striking contrast to urbane and sophisticated Harry sat Delbert, both shy and relaxed in his bib overalls. His ruddy complexion reflected his exposure to the elements as he grew up and lived his life in rural Kentucky. Delbert's hearing had been damaged in a childhood accident involving firecrackers, so he usually waited for someone to give him direct eye contact and initiate a conversation before speaking. He was happily munching a bag of popcorn from the old-fashioned popcorn machine that was always available to the residents. The aroma, the feel, and the sound of the crunching popcorn were especially comforting to Delbert.

Jack, Delbert's service dog that let him know when the phone rang or someone was knocking at his door, sat between Delbert and Patsy, completing the circle.

Missing from the group this morning was Fanny Louise, who was in the skilled nursing cottage recovering from a broken hip, and Catherine, who was reluctant to join in any group activity.

Patsy started. "Today I'm going to tell you a story. I want you to try hard to remember the details of the story, because you're going to retell it to one member of our group. Let's have Alletta and Harry go out in the hall while I tell the rest of you the story, then Harry, you'll come back in. The group will tell you the story, then when Alletta comes in you'll tell it to her." Patsy said a silent prayer that today's game wouldn't be too difficult for them, then helped Harry and Alletta out into the hall and asked them to wait until she came back for them.

Returning to her seat, Patsy continued. "Here's our story. One day, a couple was driving home from dinner on Fair Oaks Boulevard when they saw a man on the sidewalk attack a woman and take her purse. The man was tall, with black hair and a mustache. He wore green pants and a cowboy hat. He ran around the corner down Eastern Avenue and into Balboa Shores. The couple called the police and reported what they saw."

Opening the door to the hall, Patsy waved and called, "Okay Harry, why don't you come in?" Harry and Alletta hovered close together and were talking softly. "Alletta, I want you to stay put for just one more minute." Alletta's face was disappointed as Harry walked into the room without her. Harry gave Patsy a playful pat on her bum, looked at Alletta, wiggled his eyebrows, and followed Patsy back into the room.

Shutting the door, she said, "Let's start with Olga. Why don't you begin telling Harry the story."

"Well, Harry," Olga began, adjusting her glasses confidently, "this couple was coming home from dinner and they were driving down Fair Oaks Boulevard."

10

Patsy interrupted. "Good start, Olga. Maisie, can you go on from there?"

"No," whispered Maisie, looking down at her sparkly red shoes. "All I know is there were on Fair Oaks Boulevard."

"Can you remember what they saw?"

"I think they saw a car coming home from dinner." Patsy knew from the timbre of Maisie's voice that she wasn't very with it this morning.

"Very close, Maisie. They saw a man do something. What was he doing, Miss Millie?"

"Oh, that's easy," said Miss Millie. "He was grabbing her purse."

"Whose purse, Miss Millie?"

"The lady walking home from dinner."

"Oooo-kay. Beatrice, what did the man look like?" asked Patsy.

"He had dark hair and eyes and was wearing a hat, a policeman's hat."

Smiling, Patsy forged ahead trying to help the group remember a few facts from the original story. "Olga, do you remember the color of his pants?"

"Sure, they were brown. Most men's pants are brown. I prefer gray myself. More stylish than brown."

"Well, this man's pants were green," said Patsy. Her voice was beginning to take on a hint of frustration, but Patsy did her best to remain friendly. "Does anyone remember that I said they were green?" They all raised their hands.

"Delbert, your turn. What did the man do after he grabbed the purse?"

"He ran away."

"Exactly! Where did he go?"

"To the police station!" Beatrice chimed in triumphantly.

Patsy decided it was time to ditch this game and try a different one. She went to the door. "Alletta, come on in and join the group." Alletta was happy to have her seat back and happier still that the seat was next to Harry. She scooted her chair a little closer to him.

"How many of you remember playing telephone when you were little?" asked Patsy. Almost everyone's hand went up. "Good, then let's give it a try." Patsy leaned over to Olga and whispered in her ear. "Miss Millie looks great today in her nice blue dress." Olga dutifully whispered to Sarah, who in turn whispered to Miss Millie.

"Why thank you Patsy," chirped Miss Millie. "My middle daughter bought this for me just last week. But I don't think it's ice blue. It's more of a periwinkle, don't you think?"

Patsy responded with a good-natured, "Miss

Millie, I do, I do. Now, I want you to whisper what you heard to Beatrice."

"Oh, okay," said Miss Millie as she leaned over to Beatrice and whispered not so softly. Beatrice passed it on to Maisie. The chain continued until it reached Delbert.

"Delbert, how did it end up? What did you hear?" asked Patsy.

"I heard *blah, blah, blah*."

Patsy looked at Harry, who was just before Delbert in the whisper chain. "Harry, is that what you told Delbert?"

"No," Harry insisted. "I said *Millie cooks late in her nice new nest*."

"Delbert?" questioned Patsy, with a raised eyebrow.

Smiling, Delbert said in his monotone voice, "I couldn't hear anything. It sounded like *blah, blah, blah* to me."

"Okay everyone, I think that's enough for today. But remember, next week, same time same place." Patsy knew she would have to do the remembering for them. She continued in a gentler manner. "I hope you're all looking forward to our Goodbye to Summer party. There will be music, food and dancing, so plan to wear your dancing shoes."

As everyone slowly rose to leave, Harry turned

to Patsy and asked, "Can I dance with you?"

"Of course," Patsy said. "I'll save the first dance for you."

"You are my darlin'," Harry crooned.

"Ditto," Patsy called after him as he left.

Patsy went to the library and snatched several books off the shelf, then returned to the reception area where Catherine sat vigil beside her painting and satchel. To divert Catherine, Patsy "tripped" over Catherine's satchel and the books went flying silently over the plush carpet.

"Oops, I'm sorry Catherine, I didn't see your satchel. Can you help me pick up these books and take them to the library?"

Catherine stood, steadied herself, and with a straight back, silently bent to pick up each book and set them on the large foyer table. From the bouquet in the middle of the round table, the fragrance of lilacs drifted toward her and helped refocus her mind.

Walking down the hall to the library, Patsy called housekeeping to arrange for a worker to carry the painting and satchel back to Catherine's room.

"Would you like to help me shelve these books, Catherine?"

"No," was Catherine's terse answer. "I'm going to rest awhile before lunch."

Patsy watched as Catherine walked down the long hallway. Catherine paused at the shadow box beside her door. It held photos of her youth: twelve-year-old Catherine riding her horse, Opal; a cheesecake picture of her at the beach, age seventeen; one of her standing beside her father and mother in her cap and gown at her 1950 graduation from Bryn Mawr; one of her behind her desk at Apex Corporation; and several of her world travels. Missing, however, like pages ripped from a book, were Catherine's pictures of Spain.

CHAPTER 3
CATHERINE KINGSTON
SPAIN, SUMMER 1950

Born into a wealthy family, Catherine Kingston had all of the material things an only child is privileged to receive, plus summer camps and prestigious prep schools. But she led a sheltered life. Her father was president and CEO of Apex Corporation, an import-export conglomerate. Her few boarding school friends lived on the west coast and Catherine had little opportunity to make new friends at home during summer breaks. Her timid, shy manner did not endear her to her socialite mother, and she was often left alone in their New York high rise apartment. So Catherine sought refuge in the two things she loved most: reading and drawing.

She particularly liked drawing faces. She would take her artists sketchpad down to the lobby and sketch tenants as they picked up their mail. Once, after reading an art book about the lives of the great masters, Catherine asked her mother to take her to the Metropolitan Museum of Art. Surprisingly, Catherine's mother agreed. There, she discovered the modern artists and their use of bold shapes and colors. She became an ardent fan.

In college Catherine took several art courses, and decided to major in art and pursue it as a career. Her father was outraged. He considered art a hobby, not a career, and it wasn't long before he put his foot down.

"Catherine, you can't be serious," shouted her father. "You need to be sensible for once in your life. You will major in business. It will prepare you for joining the company after you graduate. That's always been the plan. It was the course I followed and it has served me well. End of discussion."

Catherine couldn't muster the strength to stand up to her father's verbal battering, and she soon buckled to her father's wishes, just as she always had. After all, she thought, business *was* more practical, and she could always pursue art as a hobby. For her college graduation, Catherine's parents gave her a trip to France, Italy, and Spain.

She was excited to be going abroad on her own. However, her excitement was short-lived when she found out her father had made all the arrangements for transportation, accommodations and (of course) chaperones. He had arranged for several of his business acquaintances to escort Catherine at each stop. They were to take her sightseeing, to art museums, the opera, and the symphony.

Catherine started her tour in Paris, where she

saw the old masters at the Louvre and the Impressionists at the Musee d'Jeu Pauma. She saw sculptures at the Rodin and attended an opera at the Paris Opera House. Although these places were both elegant and cultural, Catherine was hoping to explore the world of Matisse, Chagall and Picasso. She longed to stroll the Left Bank and spend some time in the little cabarets along the Seine.

Italy was much the same. She was escorted through Rome, Florence, and Venice by middle-aged men or their wives because, as *señor* Vincenzo, the third in a line of chaperones, admonished, "It can be very dangerous in this country for a young lady on her own."

By the time she dragged herself onto the train to Barcelona, Catherine felt like shrieking *if I hear one more opera or visit one more museum, I'll scream!*

Officially her trip was scheduled to end in Madrid, but in Barcelona the trip and her life took an unexpected turn. Her father's business contact, *señor* Casal, passed his escorting responsibility over to his nephew, who in turn passed it on to his artist friend Alejandro, whom he promised to pay.

Early on her first morning in Barcelona, Catherine sat waiting in her hotel room for her escort to arrive. Knowing the day was to be extremely hot, she wore a lightweight blue sundress. Her escort was late, but far from being upset, Catherine hoped beyond hope that he may have forgotten about her.

Checking her French twist in the mirror, she heard a knock at the door. She pulled the door open to find a handsome young Spaniard gazing back at her.

"*Hola, señorita* Kingston. My name is Alejandro Mendez. I will be your escort today." He leaned casually against the door jamb, arms folded, looking her over. "And after seeing you, I must say it is less of a chore than I expected." Startled by his familiarity, she backed away, aware of the strong heat creeping through her body.

"Where is *señor* Casal?" she asked, under the gaze of his dark liquid eyes, trying to hide the overwhelming delight that this man was most definitely not her father's stuffy business associate.

"*Señorita*, he was unavoidably detained. He asked me to take you to the *Sagrada Familia* and to see the famous works of Gaudi. I prefer Picasso and Miro, but I know enough to be the perfect guide."

"So, you're a tour guide?"

"Guide? No, I am but a poor, struggling artist."

"Oh, an artist! A modern artist." She found that fascinating, along with his dazzling good looks.

19

Mesmerized, she asked, "What medium do you use? Where do you exhibit your work?"

"Ah, *señorita*, I work mostly in oils and my home is my studio. My work has not yet had the honor of hanging in a gallery. I sell a few along the *Ramblas* on Sundays. But someday, *señorita*, someday I will be famous." He paused for a moment before continuing. "After seeing some of the city, would you like to see my paintings?"

"Yes, that sounds perfect. Let's go," she said as she closed the door behind them.

"My pleasure," he said softly, guiding Catherine outside, resting his hand gently at her waist.

Outside, to Catherine's surprise and delight, Alejandro pointed at his Vespa motor scooter. Putting his hand out to help her, he instructed her to climb on behind and hang on. Catherine laughed as she gathered her skirt around her, climbed aboard, and wrapped her arms around him. As he revved the bike to life he said, "I don't think your beautiful twist will stay up for long. Why don't you let it down now, before we start?"

Catherine took the pins out of her hair, put them in her pocket, and ran her fingers through her hair. "All right," she shouted to be heard over the engine noise, "I'm ready to go."

Riding through the streets of Barcelona, the

breeze gave Catherine relief from the heat of the day, but not from the pleasant heat of Alejandro's body. She had a sense of freedom she'd never felt before. He took her to the *Sagrada Familia*, the Gothic Quarter, and stopped at most of Gaudi's magnificent sculptures and buildings. At *Park Guell*, they sat on the grass and talked.

He asked her about her life in New York. "It must be the most exciting city in the whole world, no? I hope to go there one day myself."

"I don't think it's anything special. In fact, I find it quite dull compared to this," she said, sweeping her arms to indicate the beauty of Barcelona. "And to be able to draw and paint it all must be the most satisfying occupation on earth."

"Yes, it is what I love and I live simply. I must, because there is no money to be made unless you have a rich patron."

"It must have been wonderful growing up here. New York is so fast-paced and sterile. It can be lonely," said Catherine as she plucked blades from the grass.

"I had a beautiful childhood. Catalonia is the only place to raise children," beamed Alejandro. "The language of Catalonia is different from the rest of Spain. It is a little French and a little Spanish. Our history and culture are entirely our own. Have you been to *Las Ramblas* yet?"

"No, but what you've shown me has been incredible. I've had a wonderful day, Alejandro."

"It's not over yet. We must go to *Las Ramblas*. It is very lively at night and you promised to come see my paintings, remember? But first, I have a surprise for you back in the Gothic Quarter."

When they arrived at the Cathedral plaza, there was music and crowds of people, children, old men, old women, young men, young women, and lovers, all dancing together in a circle, clasping hands and holding them high in the air. "The *Sardana*," Alejandro explained. Catherine was enchanted with the spectacle, so full of joy and enthusiasm.

"Can we join them?" she asked.

"It is better we watch for now. There are many precise steps and only Catalonians join the circle. For us the dance is a symbol of our national identity and pride."

After watching the *Sardana*, they left the Cathedral and walked down *Las Ramblas*, stopping at flower stands, artists displays, and the outdoor market.

That evening, they lingered at a little outside cafe with candlelit tables and small vases of flowers. They ordered wine and Catherine was delighted when their server brought out a tray of tapas.

"Tapas come complimentary with the drinks," Alejandro explained.

"I've never had them before. I won't have any appetite left for dinner." When Catherine reached for one, Alejandro took her hand and kissed her palm.

"Ah, then you'll have more appetite to spend at my loft, looking at my paintings."

Catherine smiled as she withdrew her hand to pick up a tapa and pop it in her mouth. "Mmm, delicious," she murmured.

"Do this for me," asked Alejandro as he took his tongue and ran it around his lips. Catherine lowered her chin to her chest. He took hold of her chin and raised it. "Come on, for me." Looking into his soulful eyes she slowly ran her tongue around her lips.

"Mmmmm," he said.

CHAPTER 4

It took Patsy most of the afternoon to finish preparations for the end of summer dance. When finished, she went to the staff room for a few minutes to relax. After a full day she was tired, but Susan had made it clear that she was to attend, and she knew that the residents looked forward to seeing her at the party.

She laid down on the sofa and closed her eyes, drifting into a sweet semiconscious state. The sound of music starting in the Activities Room roused her from her dreamy rest. She grabbed a cup of coffee, checked her makeup, put a smile on her face, and slowly walked herself to the party.

The chairs and tables had been pushed to the side of the room to make space for dancing. Everything was decorated in a Hawaiian theme: garlands of flowers, palm trees, tropical birds. Residents roamed the room, wearing bright Hawaiian leis. Tables held trays of finger food and Hawaiian punch. A musical ensemble called The Forever Forty was playing Hawaiian music interspersed with hits from the thirties and forties. The band members were dressed in Hawaiian shirts and every head was either bald, silver, or white.

Harry approached Patsy before she had time to

say hello to anyone. "May I have this dance, Ms. Smith?"

"Why, I'd be delighted, Mr. Howell."

While they were dancing, Patsy was becoming uncomfortable. Harry was snuggling much too close, and she could feel what she thought was the surprising beginnings of an arousal. She tried to separate herself a little, but each time he pulled her close again. At the end of the dance she excused herself to get some refreshments.

"I'll get them for you, darlin'. You just sit and relax and I'll be right back."

When he left, Patsy hurried to sit with some of the other residents. "How is everyone tonight? Having fun?"

"I'm having fun," beamed Alletta. "See that young man over there? I've danced with him twice. I think I might be going home with him tonight." Glancing in the direction Alletta pointed, Patsy smiled at Danny, a young twenty-year-old Filipino caregiver, who was dancing with a wheelchair-bound resident, twirling her around and back and forth in time with the music.

"Don't be ridiculous, Alletta! He's young enough to be your son," said Catherine.

"*Much* too old for you," teased Miss Millie.

Everyone laughed. As the band started playing

Blue Hawaii, Maisie, adorned in her sparkly red shoes, stood up waving her arms and started doing a hula dance around the room. More laughter arose, and then people started to clap. *Laughter really is the best medicine*, thought Patsy.

Patsy saw Harry making his way toward her, puffing just a little from carrying two plates of food and two drinks. "I couldn't find you. You moved," he said sourly. "I thought I left you over there," he said, nodding his head toward the alcove by the dance floor. When the table erupted into laughter, Harry seemed embarrassed, but smiled his most charming smile.

"Come, Harry, sit. There's room for you by me," cooed Alletta. "Don't let us ladies scare you away."

Patsy quickly agreed. "Yes, Harry, sit and eat." After finishing one appetizer, Patsy excused herself. "I need to circulate and see that everyone's having a good time."

Harry looked hurt. "Where are you going? I thought you were my date for the night."

"No, Harry," Patsy replied. "I can't be anyone's date tonight. I'm working. You know that."

"I understand, darlin'," Harry said as he took her hand. "You have a job to do. I'll be right here if you need me."

"I'm sure you won't disappear," Patsy said as

she removed her hand and patted him lightly on the shoulder.

"Who'd want an old goat like you?" growled Catherine.

"Catherine, don't be cruel," said Miss Millie.

"Cruel? I wasn't being cruel, just honest." Catherine scanned the room slowly, as if she was expecting someone.

"I think Harry's perfectly charming," Alletta said, fluttering her eyes dramatically, silently pleading with Harry to dance with her.

Soon everyone was eating, dancing, and enjoying themselves. The fact that Harry was flirting with the other ladies now, like a bee in a flower garden, assured Patsy that the misunderstanding was long forgotten.

CHAPTER 5
CATHERINE KINGSTON
SPAIN, SUMMER 1950

After dinner they rode to Alejandro's studio. Catherine walked around the room, clutching a glass of wine, as she looked at the paintings leaning against the stark white walls of the loft.

"Beautiful, just beautiful," she gushed.

Alejandro took the glass from her hand and, taking her face in his hands, replied, "Yes, beautiful," as he kissed her softly.

When his hands moved down to draw her closer to him, she eagerly responded to his kiss, his tongue, his touch. Catherine didn't resist when he led her to his bed. Nestled in his arms, she thought *oh lord, he'll know it's my first time.* She pushed him away. "I have to tell you something."

"No need, my love. I will be gentle."

With his words giving her assurance and confidence, she let go; her passion so long repressed, it flew like a bird released from its cage. Catherine stayed the night encircled in Alejandro's strong arms.

* * *

Alejandro and Catherine spent the next week together. Seeing Spain through his eyes, so bright and full of passion, made Catherine giddy with delight. He showed her his beloved Catalonia. At Bella Beach, Catherine was surprised to see nude sunbathers lying on the hot Spanish sand. In Montserrat, they strolled along winding paths that intertwined the rough, jagged mountain. Longer trips along the Costa Brava left Catherine breathless; the views were the most beautiful she had ever seen.

Catherine checked out of her hotel and moved her belongings to Alejandro's loft. Sketch after sketch, she posed for him, feeling more beautiful than she ever had in her life. He let her pick the one she liked the best, the one she wanted him to paint.

When the day arrived for her to resume her travels and head to Madrid, where she was to end her journey, Catherine knew she was in love and had made a decision. *Señor* Casal arrived at the hotel, expecting to transport Catherine to the train station. Instead, he found Catherine seated in the lobby, a determined look on her face. "I'm not going to Madrid just yet. I'm going to stay here for a while, with Alejandro."

Señor Casal told Catherine that Mr. Kingston would not approve and that he did not want to be held responsible for her actions. "Have you called your father to ask his permission for your change of plans?"

"No, but I will. Soon," Catherine reassured him.

"Please do so right away. He can become very unpleasant when plans change without his knowledge."

Two weeks later, when *señor* Casal received a frantic call from Mr. Kingston, he learned Catherine had disregarded his advice. Mr. Kingston was very upset that he had not heard from her for well over a week. He had called her hotel in Madrid, only to find that Catherine had never checked in.

Dreading this conversation, *señor* Casal spoke calmly. "Yes, Mr. Kingston, Catherine is still here. She was supposed to call you about her change of plans."

"Change of plans? What change of plans? Are you telling me you didn't take her to the train?"

"No, *señor*, she wanted to stay in Barcelona a little while longer," *señor* Casal explained.

Mr. Kingston cut in. "What she wants is not the issue here. She has a schedule to keep and your job was to help her keep it. What is going on here?"

Señor Casal sighed and filled Mr. Kingston in on the details. Catherine's father demanded the name and phone number of the young artist.

"His name is Alejandro Mendez. He does not

have a telephone."

"What's his address then? Let him know that if I don't hear from her today, I'll be on my way there to bring her home myself."

"Yes, yes, just a moment please..." *Señor* Casal shuffled some papers on his desk. "May I call you back, *señor*? I must get the address from my nephew."

Within the hour, *señor* Casal returned the call. "His address is Barcelona, Moreto, 9. Mr. Kingston, please, is there anything more I can do to help?"

"Yes, you can go to this Moreto 9 and make sure Catherine's okay. And tell her to call me immediately."

"Of course, sir. I'll take care of it right away."

Flustered, *señor* Casal hung up the phone, locked his door, and hurried to the loft. Banging on the front door, he was met by Alejandro dressed in only his jeans; no shirt, no shoes. Catherine stood behind him. When she saw who was at the door, she pulled her flimsy robe closer and tied the sash in a tight knot.

Señor Casal pushed past Alejandro and made his way inside. Inside, the heavy wooden table was covered with bread, cheese, and fruit. It appeared that he was interrupting a late breakfast. He stomped across the room and pounded on the table, knocking the bread knife to the floor.

He directed his tirade to Catherine. "Your father called and is irate. Why did you not contact him? He doesn't know your whereabouts and sent me to find you." Catherine sat back in her chair and wrapped her arms tightly around herself. Señor Casal turned to Alejandro.

"Alejandro, you *pendejo*! You have ruined my business. Her father said if he didn't hear from her today, he was coming to get her. So, my dear lady," señor Casal continued as he leaned across the table and shook his finger at Catherine, "you need to call your father now! Not later. Not soon. Right now. Do you hear me?"

Incensed at her father's interference, Catherine stood. "Yes, I hear you, señor Casal. And thank you for relaying my father's message. I'll take care of it. Now if you'll excuse us, we are going to finish our breakfast." Catherine walked across the room and opened the front door.

Señor Casal left, slamming the door behind him, cursing all the way to his car.

* * *

Catherine went downstairs to the shop below Alejandro's loft and called home. "Hello, Father?

Yes, I'm okay. No, I'm not coming home just yet. I quite like Barcelona and I've decided to stay for a while."

"Oh no you're not, young lady. You get yourself back here right now or I'll come and get you. I know about you and this, this *artist*, and I'll not have it." Mr. Kingston's voice grew louder. "Let me speak to him. Now!" Catherine was about to hang up the phone when Alejandro took it from her.

"Hello, Mr. Kingston, my name is Alejandro Mendez. Catherine is fine. You do not have to worry about her. I have invited her to stay with me and extend her visit."

"I'm not worried, I'm furious," responded her father. "Either you see that she is on the next plane home, or I will come and get her, and I assure you it will not be pleasant for you. Now put Catherine back on." Alejandro held the receiver out to Catherine, nodding his head toward it.

"Yes, Father?"

"Catherine, if you don't stop this foolishness and come home now, I will be forced to take matters into my own hands. Do you understand?"

"Yes, Father, I understand."

"Good. Then when can I expect you?"

"I said I understand, Father. I didn't say I was coming home." Catherine gently put down the receiver.

Alejandro took her in his arms as tears flooded her eyes. "He's always controlled everyone around him, including me. Well, he won't control me anymore." She leaned against his chest. "He doesn't care about me or my happiness. He only cares about keeping me under his control." Alejandro held her awhile, nuzzling her hair, taking in its sweet freshness.

A few days later, Catherine took the early train to Girona to explore the possibility of starting classes at the university and obtaining a degree in Art History. Alejandro stayed behind to finish a painting for a small commission from an important client. He awoke to the sound of someone beating against his door. "Yes, yes, I'm coming." Alejandro stumbled to the door and opened it, to find a well-dressed man in a business suit. "Can I help you?" he mumbled.

"I am Franklin Hughes. I represent Mr. Kingston. May I come in?"

Rubbing his hands over his face to wake up, Alejandro muttered, "Yes, come in. Please excuse the way I look." He was still wearing his old painting jeans from the night before and his hair was rumpled. It was evident he hadn't shaved for several days. "I was up late painting," he explained as he opened the door wider. With a gallant sweep of his hand, he let Mr. Hughes in.

"Is Catherine here?"

"No, she's gone to Girona for the day."

"Good, that makes what I have to say easier."

"Please sit down, Mr. Hughes. And tell me what it is you have to say." Alejandro offered a chair but Mr. Hughes remained standing. "No thanks. I'll make this quick. Mr. Kingston is ready to offer you a tidy sum to cut all ties to Catherine."

"What?" Alejandro's knees went weak as he slumped into a chair. "This man, Mr. Kingston, wants to pay me not to see his daughter?"

"No, I said cut all ties with her, Mr. Mendez. Ten thousand dollars is a considerable amount of money."

"Ten thousand dollars? Are you mad? Absolutely not. Who in his right mind offers ten thousand dollars to destroy his daughter's happiness? Rich Americans! I can't believe it. He must be even more of a bastard than Catherine said. Does Catherine know about this?"

Holding his briefcase in front of him, Mr Hughes squared his jaw before answering. "No, she's not to know anything about this."

"You cannot pay me money to give up Catherine. I love her and she loves me."

"Mr. Kingston doesn't deal in love. He deals in

cold, hard cash."

"Well, you tell Mr. Kingston I'm not dealing."

"I'm afraid refusing is not an option. I've been advised to up the ante if there's a problem. Fifteen thousand?" Alejandro looked down and shook his head. Mr. Hughes continued, "Twenty thousand?"

Stunned, Alejandro looked the man in the eye, and finding nothing there but cold determination, pummeled his fists against the table, then put his head down and wept.

When Catherine returned that evening, Alejandro kissed her gently before he spoke. "Catherine, I've given this much thought. I cannot let you give up everything for an uncertain future with me. I can't provide the kind of life you are used to. I can hardly provide for myself some days. I don't want to be the one who destroys your relationship with your father. One day you would resent me for what you gave up, and I could never forgive myself for that." He took her hands and put his forehead to hers. His eyes were dark and tender, his voice choked with emotion. "You need to go home. I will come to get you, soon, I promise. I will make myself more acceptable to your father, and then I will come. *Cara mia*, take the painting and hold it as a promise."

She argued passionately, but Alejandro held

firm. In the end, Catherine went home, trusting that Alejandro would come for her.

CHAPTER 6
OCTOBER

The liquid amber outside the windows of Howell Construction glistened like a garnet as sunshine hit the rain-slicked leaves, but all was not so bright inside. Casey Howell sat behind his desk, feet up, holding the telephone between his ear and his shoulder, talking to his sister. He fidgeted with a pencil, sliding his fingers down to the end and then turning it over and repeating the action. As usual, the topic of conversation was their father.

"Says he wants to get married. The old coot thinks he's in love. He told me yesterday when I went to see him. He calls her 'darlin' and says we'll love her when we meet her."

Casey held the phone away from his ear as his sister shrieked. "Married?! We can't go through this again. Married, my ass."

"I know, I feel the same way. I'm going to see the woman who runs Balboa Shores and ask her which gold digger's got Dad in her clutches now. She told me on the phone she didn't know anything about it. She said he's an adult and still legally responsible for his decisions."

Another explosion came from the other end of the line. "Did you tell her how he's been led by the nose down the matrimonial aisle before? Tell her he doesn't make good decisions and he's easily persuaded by beautiful women. You better be on their backs about this or you damn well know what could happen."

"I know, but I'm still nervous. I'll be sure to give her the run down when I see her. I did tell her that Dad doesn't always know when he's being played. Ms. Jackson said she would try to see if he was serious about anyone, but if I wanted to make decisions about his life I would need to gain conservatorship. I told her she better do more than try to find out who this woman is and protect my father from being exploited. We may have to consider getting legal advice." As he ended the call and put down the phone, Casey pondered the fact that his dad seemed to be dipping into the cup of senility a bit more each and every day.

*   *   *

The rain was coming down heavily and Patsy's old wiper blades couldn't keep up. The traffic between the college and Balboa Shores was congested and she knew she was going to be late for work. When she finally arrived, a white pickup truck cut her off and pulled into the last staff parking spot. Written on its side in large black letters was HOWELL AND SON CONSTRUCTION COMPANY. Patsy blasted her horn, but the man getting out of the truck ignored it.

She rolled down her window and yelled at him, "Hey, can't you read? The sign says STAFF PARKING. I was going to park there."

The man paused a moment, looked her straight in the eye, then pulled his baseball cap down tight by the bill and made a dash for the entrance. *What a jerk,* Patsy thought. But then again, there weren't many men like Bud. She'd been lucky.

Patsy drove around to the visitor lot and parked her car. Groping around in the back seat for an umbrella, she retrieved a magazine, a binder, and myriad papers, but no umbrella. In her rush she'd probably left it in her last class. *Hurry hurry, round and round, such is the hamster wheel of my life.* Grabbing the binder, she held it over her head as she raced inside. As she passed the boss's door, she noticed the man from the white pickup truck talking fast and furious to Ms. Jackson. *Well, let's see her earn her money,* thought Patsy.

Patsy continued on to the Activities Room where she was scheduled to lead a watercolor class after lunch. Balboa Shores encouraged its residents to stay as active as possible, both mentally and physically, and painting was one of Patsy's favorite classes to lead. She covered the table with newspaper and got out the round plastic palettes that looked like deviled egg holders. At each place, she set two cups of water, a paint set, a paintbrush, and a paper towel. Today's picture was a rose that Patsy had pre-drawn on watercolor paper. She was looking forward to teaching what little she knew about watercolor techniques to the group.

After lunch, residents started arriving one by one. Patsy never knew how many would show up. Sometimes a resident was ill or just plain forgot. Others came only because their caregiver took the time to bring them.

She started by explaining, "You don't use watercolors like crayons or oil paint. You let the water do the work." Demonstrating as she spoke, Patsy continued, "First we're going to paint only one petal at a time with plain water. Then we'll add some paint to the water on the petal. You don't want to outline the petal or fill it in with solid color. We are going to put the red watercolor along the inside at the base of the petal. It should spread to the rest of the petal by itself. The color becomes paler and paler as it flows to the outside edge. This gives the petal depth."

When everyone had finished one petal, Patsy

continued. "Pick another petal that is not touching the wet one and paint it just with water first. If two petals that are wet touch each other, they'll run together and you'll get a huge mess. Once a petal is dry, you can paint the one next to it." She watched as the group accomplished this task with varying levels of competence. "Keep doing this until you've painted all the petals."

She observed the residents as they worked. Three painted each petal separately, but filled them in as if they were using crayon. One painted the whole rose without making any distinction between petals. Maisie said, "I've painted the mouth and eyes, but I don't see the ears."

Patsy smiled and continued encouraging the budding artists, telling each of them they were doing fine. When Beatrice said, "Hers is better than mine," Patsy replied, "One is not better, Beatrice, just different. That's what art is all about – interpretation."

After painting the leaves and stem, Patsy demonstrated how to speckle gold paint to make the rose look antique. "Speckling hides a multitude of flaws."

Harry, the lone man in the group, had gone over and over his flower from top to bottom with brown paint, until it soaked through the paper onto the table. Little of the red and green showed through, and when he added the gold, it looked like an abstract painting ... of what, Patsy couldn't decide. "I'm not very artistic, I'm afraid," mused Harry. "I just came to be with my darlin' Patsy."

Maisie added green spikes at the top of her painting for hair, making a bizarre image even stranger. The others produced recognizable roses.

"The final step," Patsy concluded, "is framing. Framing always makes a painting look more professional." The white tag-board mats did improve the finished look, Patsy thought, as she added names to each and pinned them on the bulletin board. "Good job, everyone!"

She looked up and saw Susan Jackson standing in the door, watching. Susan always made Patsy feel uneasy. They were about the same age, both single, Susan by choice, Patsy by pain. Susan was cool and aloof, prim and proper with her slim figure and dark hair bobbed just above her shoulders.

Of course she has confidence, Patsy thought. *She has an Ivy League education while I'm still struggling to complete community college.* Patsy noticed Susan twist and rub her neck, then rearrange the silk shirt collar over her navy blue suit jacket.

Geez, she must have had a hard day, thought

43

Patsy sarcastically. Patsy's day had already included both school and work, and there would be homework in the evening.

"Patsy, may I see you in my office for a moment?" asked Susan.

"Sure, just let me clean up here first, and I'll be right in."

On her way to Ms. Jackson's office, Patsy noticed Catherine once again keeping a lookout by the front doors.

"Please close the door behind you," Susan said. "Casey Howell, Harry's son, came to see me this morning. He's concerned that Harry is getting seriously involved with someone here at Balboa Shores to the point of considering marriage. His father won't tell him who it is, only that she his 'darlin' and he'll introduce her when the time is right. Do you know who he may be talking about?"

"Harry calls everyone darlin', including me, so it's hard to tell. He was flirting with several women the other night at the dance."

"Did he seem to be giving anyone particular attention?"

Patsy remembered her dance with Harry at the end of summer party. She told Susan about Harry's flirtation, but left out the part about his arousal.

"Thank you for making me aware of the

44

situation, Patsy. Please be extra careful that you don't give Harry any encouragement."

"I haven't, Ms. Jackson, honestly."

Susan frowned at Patsy. "It looks like this could be a real problem, Miss Smith. If I receive any direct evidence that you have enticed Harry in any way, we could be sued and it would also be grounds for your dismissal. Do we understand each other?"

"Perfectly, Ms. Jackson." Patsy turned and left the office without another word. *I can't believe after all the years I've been here, she thinks I would be as unprofessional as to encourage a romance with a resident! Now I have to deal with Harry's delusional romance along with everything else on my plate.*

Feeling a little touchy, Patsy spotted Catherine and approached her. "Catherine, I need your opinion on some paintings. Will you come with me to the Activities Room?" Catherine's judgmental temperament was piqued, and she followed Patsy to the bulletin board which held the rose paintings.

"Which one do you think is best?" asked Patsy.

"There is no best. None of these are real art."

"Okay Catherine, why don't you show me some real art? I bet you have some in your room. I'll walk with you and you can show me." Catherine started toward her room with purpose.

CHAPTER 7
CATHERINE KINGSTON
NEW YORK, SPRING 1950

Catherine's flight arrived in New York after midnight. She checked into the Plaza Hotel at Fifth Avenue and 59th Street in Manhattan. She washed her face, plopped into bed, and fell into a restless sleep. In the morning, she called room service for coffee and croissants and nibbled while overlooking Central Park. Feeling somewhat fortified, she dialed her parents.

"Where the hell are you, Catherine?" her father asked.

"I'm in New York at the Plaza, where I will stay until I find a place to live in the city."

"Your home is here, with your mother and me. It's not safe for you in the city alone. You've proven that this summer."

"No, Father, I'm not coming home. You forced me to come back, and I'll work in the business, but I'll be damned if I'll live under your roof. I am not your little girl anymore. I am going to live on my own. I'll look for an apartment this week." She hung up before Mr. Kingston could respond.

Catherine found a modest brownstone apartment in Greenwich Village on Charlton Street.

The two-bedroom had good north and south light, which was important since the space would double as Alejandro's studio when he arrived. She hung the nude portrait that Alejandro had given her over the sofa in the living room. Keeping in line with the rest of her quirky Village neighbors, Catherine furnished the place with an eclectic assortment of thrift store finds.

As promised, Catherine began working for her father as an assistant to the vice president of the advertising department. She filled her spacious office with beautiful furniture, a wet bar, flowers, and art. *The more expensive, the better* became Catherine's motto. Her father could certainly afford it. She avoided him as much as possible, communicating mostly in memos and terse interoffice phone calls. Her mother phoned at least once a week to invite her to dinner, but Catherine never accepted. After putting in her day at the office, she would hurry back to her apartment and quickly change out of her work clothes and into tights with a black turtleneck sweater.

Catherine spent her nights painting and writing long love letters to Alejandro. Expecting to receive similar letters filled with love and devotion, she checked her mailbox every evening, only to be disappointed day after day. For weeks she wrote and never received a response, and Catherine often fell asleep crying into her pillow, her heart hurting for just one word from him. Where were all the beautiful words and the promises he made? Where was her beloved Alejandro? What had happened to him? She knew something was wrong, but she kept writing.

As weeks passed, she wrote less frequently; as months passed, her letters became less personal. She became disillusioned, not just with Alejandro, but with her own memories of their time together. She came to believe that his love, this love, any romantic love, was just a fantasy.

Catherine handled her disillusionment by immersing herself in her job. She convinced her father that she could promote the placement of Jackson Pollock-style art in offices of company executives, law offices, and other commercial venues in the city. Expanding the breadth of his corporation and his wealth always appealed to her father, and he allowed her to do it on a trial basis. In her Village neighborhood she discovered young new artists who were eager to sell their art at bargain prices. She developed a separation from her work that allowed her to sleep with many of these young artists, never letting the two worlds intertwine.

The placing of art in office buildings became very successful. Catherine became a savvy negotiator, placing pieces with customers at a significant profit. Many attractive, successful, professional men took an interest in Catherine Kingston, heir to the Apex Corporation, including Franklin Hughes, her father's attorney and confidant. But she held them all at bay with cool detachment. She moved into a trendy loft in Soho. Surrounded herself with expensive trappings, and felt she had at last proven herself in the eyes of her father.

* * *

The telephone in Catherine's apartment rang early one morning. On the line her mother's voice was panic-stricken. "Catherine, your father … your father … he's had a heart attack. We're on our way to Mt. Sinai Hospital. I need you … and Franklin. Have him meet us at the hospital. Hurry please."

Franklin, thought Catherine. Yes, of course, Franklin. He's always there when Father needs him. "All right, Mother, don't worry. Father will make it through. He's tough." She hung up and called Franklin, then, not wanting to wait for a company car, hailed a taxi.

By the time Catherine arrived at the hospital, her father was gone. She found her mother standing in the emergency room looking frail, old, and oh so alone. Catherine reached a tentative arm out, and her mother collapsed into her arms, quietly sobbing. She was trying to console her mother when Franklin arrived and took over. Catherine was glad he was there for support.

Franklin stayed by her side the next few days and helped make funeral arrangements as her mother, for all her prior strength, was now ineffectual.

A week after the funeral, Catherine and her mother were in Franklin Hughes' office for the reading of the will. Franklin began, "Judith, of course Richard looked after you. All the real property is yours and he set up a generous trust for you for the rest of your life.

"Catherine, he left the company to you in trust. That means that you own it, but you do not have complete control at this time. He designated me as co-trustee. Along with the board of directors, we will guide you until such time as you marry. Then your husband will become co-trustee with you, with the approval of the board of directors."

"Will I be able to make decisions for this company I own?"

"Yes and no. You will need the approval of the co-trustee and the board of directors for any major decisions."

"So my father never intended for me to run the company, is that correct? I'm to be a figurehead with no real authority?"

"I don't think Richard thought that a woman, any woman, could make important decisions. He left it to you in trust, so let's just work with that for the time being and see what we can do to change it later."

Judith Kingston spoke up for the first time. "Franklin, could you give Catherine and me a few minutes alone please?"

"Certainly, Mrs. Kingston. I'll be just down the hall."

After Franklin left the office, a defeated-looking Judith spoke. "Catherine, there is something I need to share with you. Leaving the company to you in trust was your father's final humiliation to me and to you. He didn't trust me to have it and he didn't want me to have any influence over you. So he bypassed us both by leaving everything in a trust, to be run by Franklin."

Since her father's death, her mother had been depressed and not herself. "What are you talking about, Mother?"

"I know you're confused but that's because you

don't know some details of our family history. Your father has been overprotective and indulgent of you all your life, so that no one would have a reason to think he didn't love you. But, when you went to Spain and fell in love, he was overwhelmed with jealousy and anger. That's when he put the company into trust upon his death. He thought history was going to repeat itself."

Catherine was weary. "I still don't understand, Mother. This is making no sense."

Judith took her daughter's hand. "When we were newly married, your father was often away on business. He was trying to build a secure financial future for us, but that didn't soothe my feelings of loneliness. We had an Italian gardener who wrote beautiful poetry. Marcos gave me attention, but more important, he gave me his time. I would sit in the garden and he would recite his poetry while he worked. Then one day he told me he had a special poem. It was about his desire for me, and it was beautiful. He found me desirable. *Me*. And I responded. By the time your father found out, I was pregnant. He never forgave me, and though he treated me the same in public, any true feelings he had for me were long gone. His pride would never let him admit that his wife had an affair that produced a child.

"He didn't want anyone to think that your parentage was in doubt, so he spoiled you and gave you every advantage that he could. When you started to show an interest in the arts, he quickly made sure your road to that future was closed. He made you dependent on him. When you were in Spain, your independence threatened him. Catherine, in leaving the company to you in trust he was trying to hurt me and keep you under his control."

Angry now, Catherine paced back and forth. She fumed, "It explains a lot. Why he could be so generous to me and then turn around and be so unreasonable and cruel." Glaring now at her mother, Catherine spat, "Why didn't you tell me this years ago when I first came home from Spain?"

"I thought you were too young, and then later, I was afraid you might hate your father and me."

"Oh, Mother, I couldn't hate you. It's true we haven't been close. That's because I thought you agreed with him on everything. I didn't know why he was so hard on me, but I never had any idea that I wasn't his flesh and blood."

"He's gone now, so there's nothing more he can do to us." Her mother sighed as she opened the door to the hall. "We should call Franklin back in and finish this business. But first, are you okay?"

"I will be. I do have one question, though. Why did you stay with him all these years? Why didn't you leave him for your lover? You did love Marcos, didn't you?"

Judith turned toward Catherine. She shook her head and wiped away tears. "Of course I did. But it was complicated. I still loved your father. Marcos was just there at the right – or possibly the worst – time. I suppose I didn't know enough about love to decide whom I loved more, or why. So I took the easiest way out. I chose the known over the unknown, the safe way."

"The safe way meaning financially?" asked Catherine.

"There was that, yes. And safe meaning I wanted to avoid scandal. At that point I still loved your father, I just wanted and needed more from him." Judith sighed heavily. "Forgive me, Catherine. I should have shared this with you a long time ago. I'm glad you know the whole story, but I'm tired. I just want to put an end to this and go home."

After putting Judith into a limousine, Catherine and Franklin left the building together.

"Are you all right?" asked Franklin. "You look pale. You look like you've seen a ghost."

"I have." Feeling faint, she leaned on Franklin. "Mother and Father's marriage was a ghost, a ghost

I hope I never have to see again."

"Catherine, it's been a long, hard day. You need to relax and let someone else take care of you for a while. Let me take you to dinner. We can have a drink or two and take the edge off. What do you say?"

"Thanks, Franklin, but I'm exhausted. I really need to go home and get some rest and think about everything I've just learned. I never really knew my father at all."

CHAPTER 8

After a long work day, Patsy pulled into the Safeway parking lot to pick up a few groceries. It had taken her some time to get used to cooking for just one, but she was determined to get on a healthy diet and stay on it. That meant cooking at home instead of picking up something at the local Taco Bell after work. She liked to cook, however, she always had way too much left over. She hated to waste food, and she was tired of eating the same thing for days on end. A few months ago she tried freezing leftovers, but it was too easy to forget about all that Tupperware in the freezer. She ended up throwing out food that had once been perfectly good but had since collected a dusting of freezer burn.

Immersed in making a mental grocery list, Patsy didn't notice Brenda Brownlee, an acquaintance from school, frantically waving from her car. "Hey Patsy," Brenda yelled. "I was going to call you when I got home tonight. Some of the girls from class are going out Saturday night to Denim and Diamonds. I'd really like you to go with us."

Patsy hesitated. "I don't know, BB. I'm kind of a homebody these days. I'm just not into the bar scene."

Brenda interrupted. "It's more of a dance club than a bar. They teach line dancing and Texas two-step for those who don't know how, and there are plenty of good dance partners to go around. The atmosphere is really friendly. It's just going to be a group of ladies. You'll have fun, I promise. How 'bout it?"

"Let me think about it, okay? I'll let you know before Saturday."

"Okay girl. But have I told you lately that you need to get out more?"

Feeling the need to get away, Patsy cut the conversation short. "I'll call you, BB. I'm on a tight schedule right now."

* * *

To Patsy, the entrance to Balboa Shores was very serene and perhaps even a little romantic. *Ah, romance.* Romance reminded her of Bud. He'd been gone three years now. *Maybe it's time to start dating again.* All day Patsy pondered BB's invitation. A night out with the girls might be a good thing. She liked country music, and she and Bud had been known to trip the light fantastic a time or two in their day. She would give Brenda's invitation some serious thought.

Patsy was on her way to Miss Millie's room when Olga popped her head out of her room. "What time is it?" Olga asked.

"Seven o'clock, Olga. Time for breakfast." Patsy continued to Miss Millie's apartment.

"Miss Millie, how are you feeling this morning?"

"After the night I've had, I'm glad to be alive!" said Miss Millie, looking up from her newspaper.

"Gracious, Miss Millie, what happened?"

"Someone walked into my bedroom and climbed in bed with me last night, that's what happened!"

Patsy almost choked trying not to laugh. "Do you know who it was, Miss Millie? I can think of many residents that would like to, but few who would."

"I didn't know what was happening at first. The person came into the bedroom and just stood for a minute. I wasn't really awake. I thought it could be someone trying to wake me for some medicine or something. When the intruder turned back the covers and crawled in, I woke up real fast, I'll tell you that."

"And who did it turn out to be?" asked Patsy, sure that it had been just a dream.

Folding her newspaper, Miss Millie answered. "It was that crazy Beatrice. She kept scooting over until I was almost off the bed, and she pulled all the covers off me. I used my call button and called for help." Slapping her lap with the newspaper, she continued. "I could have fallen out of bed and broken my hip. I kept telling her to scoot over and get out of my bed, but she didn't. Finally, Judy, or Julia or or Julie... oh, one of them came in and rescued me."

Patsy sat on the edge of the sofa. "Is this the first time this has happened?"

"No, she's wandered in here before but at least that was in the daytime. Judy said Beatrice must have gotten up to go to the toilet, got confused, and ended up here in my bed."

"Here I thought you were going to tell me it was a man," Patsy chuckled.

"A man? I wish it had been a man! At least then I wouldn't have been in bed with a crazy woman. I'll tell you I was scared to death. I hardly slept the rest of the night." Miss Millie, her eyes dancing, looked at Patsy, and they both burst out laughing.

"It seems silly, now that I think about it." chortled Miss Millie. "I suppose we shouldn't be laughing at Beatrice, but it *is* pretty funny."

"We're not laughing at her, Miss Millie, we're laughing at the situation. I can just see you sitting up in bed, pushing Beatrice then pushing your call button, pushing Beatrice then pushing your call button. Bea is lucky that it was you she chose to spend the night with and not one of our grouchier residents."

On her way back from Miss Millie's, Patsy encountered Olga again. "What time is it, Patsy?" Patsy patiently gave Olga the new time and suggested that Olga walk down to breakfast with her. Olga agreed.

Olga had inherited the nickname "Cuckoo Lady" from the staff because she was like a cuckoo clock in reverse, constantly popping out of her room to ask the time in her lilting Swedish accent whenever she heard someone pass by.

Patsy walked with Olga to her table in the dining room. "Don't forget we have senior trivia this morning."

"I'll be there," said Olga.

Looking at Catherine, Patsy said, "You too, Catherine. In the Activities Room after breakfast."

When everyone had arrived for trivia except Catherine, Patsy went looking for her. Catherine sat in the chair by the front door.

"Come on, Catherine, let's go do something fun!" Patsy took Catherine's hands and steadily lifted her out of the big chair. "We have senior trivia this morning, remember? Who's tall and attractive whose name starts with C?"

"Carlos," replied Catherine.

Patsy smiled. "I was thinking Catherine, but Carlos will do."

Patsy held Catherine's hand as she led her back to the Activities Room. "Sorry for the delay, everyone." Letting go of Patsy's hand, Catherine made her way into the room. There wasn't a chair next to Sarah, so Catherine, who always liked sitting next to Sarah, had to take the end chair next to Beatrice.

"Sarah, you should have saved a chair for me," barked Catherine.

"I'm sorry, Catherine," Sarah replied in her meek voice.

Beatrice, looking askew, said, "Well, don't think I saved this chair for *you*, Catherine."

"Have a seat, Catherine, and we'll get started," said Patsy. "Alletta, what is a word for two sets of lips touching that starts with a K?"

"Cabbage," replied Alletta.

"Not quite." Patsy tried again. "When you want to show affection for someone, you k-k-k them."

"You kiss them," giggled Alletta.

Patsy smiled. "That's it! Good job, Alletta." She looked around the room and continued. "Whose name starts with A, and she went through a mirror?"

Harry's hand went up. "Alletta."

"Alletta, did you go through a mirror?" Patsy

teased. "Good try, Harry. But this was a little girl who also fell down a rabbit hole."

"I don't know any little girls," said Harry.

"It's a fairy tale you might have read as a child," coaxed Patsy.

"I don't know any fairies either."

"Who thinks they know the answer?" No hands went up. "She lived in Wonderland." No response.

"Alice," Patsy said. "Alice in Wonderland."

Patsy heard a collective "Oooooh."

* * *

After the disappointing trivia session, Patsy went to the Great Room to set up for balloon volleyball. The Great Room was covered in the same extra-thick carpet as the foyer, and all the furniture was padded, which was good for volleyball in case anyone lost their balance. Balloon volleyball was originally scheduled for after lunch, but Patsy found the residents more inclined to try the game in the mornings when they were fresh. The sport was a big hit with the women, but Patsy found the men harder to entice. She assumed having played all kinds of sports in their youth, they didn't find volleyball to be macho enough. She would need to approach them individually.

"Come on, join us, we need you." She used to put her arm through the man's arm and tug him gently toward the Great Room, cooing, "Come on, you know you really want to." It seemed to work, but since her talk with Ms. Jackson about Harry Howell, Patsy had given up this tactic.

The residents stood in a circle while they batted the balloon up into the air and over to the other players. There was no net involved and no score or sides in this game. It was all goodhearted fun and a little exercise. Sarah stood quietly and rarely tried to hit the balloon. She might catch it once in a while and then gently bat it to Catherine. Catherine usually sat and observed from one of the easy chairs, a barely disguised look of disdain on her wrinkled face. Sometimes she put a balloon between her hands and popped it (just for spite, Patsy reckoned). Maisie swung with all her might every time the balloon was in the air, her hands flailing, not even close to the balloon. "Missed by a mile," heckled Alletta as Maisie almost fell over backwards onto the sofa. "Get the butterfly!" yelled Maisie, prancing up and down in her pink ballet slippers.

"If the balloon's out of reach, let it go," coached Patsy. "We want to have fun, not broken bones." Whenever a balloon met its fateful demise, Sarah put her hands over her ears, trembling with fright at the loud popping sound. In her youth, Sarah had been a missionary in India, and the noise reminded her of gunfire, riots, and other chaos during the separation of Pakistan from India.

After about twenty minutes, everyone was exhausted and Patsy called an end to the game. "Time for some refreshments," said Patsy as the kitchen staff brought in lemonade, iced tea, and an assortment of cookies.

Susan Jackson called Patsy into her office for the second time in as many weeks. Patsy stepped into the office and, seeing the rude man who had taken her parking spot last week sitting in the guest chair, immediately tensed up.

"Patsy, this is Casey Howell. His father is Harry Howell."

Casey was stiff and formal as he shook her hand, giving Patsy a look of cynical recognition.

"Casey is worried about his father. I told him about the misunderstanding you had with Harry at the dance, and he wants to know more about your involvement."

Patsy turned to Casey and spoke in a business-like manner. "I don't have any involvement with Harry, other than in my role as caregiver."

Casey interrupted. "Are you the one he calls his

darlin'?"

Patsy bristled. "Harry calls almost everyone darlin'. So I'd say no, I'm not his darlin'."

"But he does flirt with you, correct? And you flirt with him?"

"Harry is definitely a flirt, that's true. But I don't flirt back. I'm quite fond of your father, that's all. Harry flirts with all the women at Balboa Shores. At the dance, he was flirting with Alletta and the rest of her posse. I can assure you, I'm not attracted to nor involved with Harry."

"So you might not be interested in him romantically. But I bet his money is very attractive."

"Mr. Howell, I don't make it a point to know the gross income of our residents. I am a professional and, quite frankly, I'm insulted that you would even suggest I would take advantage of your father for his money."

"Well, he plans to marry *someone*," Casey said as he stood up. "Someone he calls darlin' and I need to know who the gold digger is that's trying to get her hands on his money." His voice was forceful now. "Miss Jackson, I insist that you find out who it is."

Susan stood and put her hand out to end the meeting. "Mr. Howell, we will do what we can. Patsy, please keep an eye out for anyone to whom

Harry seems to be giving extra attention."

"Why don't you just ask him?" exclaimed Patsy.

"Because he's a stubborn old goat and he won't tell us!" shouted Casey.

"He's not stubborn. He's very charming and sweet. I'm sure you're making more out of this than it actually is," said Patsy.

"How would you know? Have you had to go to court to prove a marriage isn't legal because your father is incapable of consummating it? Dad's here because his live-in caregiver whisked him off to Las Vegas, and I don't want to go through that again."

Patsy was speechless. She was reasonably certain Harry was not impotent. She was sorry Harry had been taken advantage of by a woman from his past, but his son was reacting like a lunatic. Casey was nothing like his father. *How did Harry spawn an idiot like this?*

The encounter sent Patsy's healthy eating intentions right out the door. At home, she put on one of Bud's old shirts and flopped down on the couch with a burger and fries. Bud was gone. There was no way he was coming back. She missed him. She wrapped her arms around herself. As long as she stayed this way, she could smell him; she could almost feel his touch. She wanted to hold onto Bud for as long as possible.

CHAPTER 9
CATHERINE KINGSTON
NEW YORK, SPRING 1959

After her father's death, Catherine accepted her role as co-trustee with Franklin and enjoyed the perks she attained as the figurehead of Apex Corporation. Love came only by way of her cat, Maurice. Not unconditional love, as Maurice could be cool and haughty, but when he was willing to be cuddled and petted, she found in him at least comfort if not love.

Catherine by necessity was in close and frequent contact with Franklin Hughes. He conferred with her and listened to her business ideas with respect. He took her to dinner meetings and offered professional advice when asked. They discovered they shared a love of art and opera. He was intelligent, kind, gentlemanly, and she began to look forward to his company.

Maurice was sitting on Catherine's lap one evening as she sipped a glass of Chardonnay. She watched the news as she distractedly ran her hands over his fur. The phone rang and, in no hurry, she picked up the receiver. "Hello, Catherine Kingston speaking."

"Catherine, this is Franklin. Forgive me for

interrupting your evening, but I received the new season schedule for the opera today and thought I would find out if you would like to accompany me, and which ones you might be interested in."

Catherine put down her wine and pushed Maurice off her lap. She held the phone with both hands and surprised herself with her answer. "You're not interrupting anything important, Franklin. Thank you for thinking of me. What is scheduled for this season?" He read through the list of six performances. "I like all of them," she replied.

"Then it's settled. We'll see them all. I'll get two season tickets and we'll make it a standing date."

That sounds wonderful, Franklin. I look forward to it."

"The first one is *Traviata*. Two weeks from now. We can plan to have dinner beforehand if that's okay with you."

"That would be lovely. Thank you so much."

* * *

Two years later Catherine agreed to marry Franklin Hughes. A man for whom she held enormous respect, but little passion. After their marriage, the board of trustees turned complete control over to Catherine and Franklin – knowing he held a strong influence over her and would be around to advise her, and would be her beneficiary.

Trusting Catherine's business sense, Franklin felt free to start his own law firm. The marriage was a sensible partnership, a win-win for them both, the best part of both worlds.

Their life was filled with work, opera, travel, and social commitments, but no children. Catherine was happy, her life was comfortable, and she was content with that. So what if true love passed her by? She thought passion was overrated anyway.

*   *   *

One spring morning, the smell of fresh coffee greeted Catherine as she made her way to the kitchen. Franklin was seated reading his paper. As she bent over to kiss the top of his head, she glanced down at the article he was reading. The headline announced *Alejandro Mendez brings his art to New York*. Her heart started pounding. *Could it be? Could it really be him?*

Pouring her coffee, she took her time adding cream and sugar and then sat down across from Franklin. "What's happening in the news this morning?" she asked.

Franklin moved the paper down and took a sip of

coffee. "Nothing much my dear, just the same dreary topics we read about every day." Looking at his watch, he stood, folded the paper, and put it in his briefcase. "A driver is picking me up early this morning. Take your time getting ready. I'll have him come back later for you." Catherine stood and, with a quick perfunctory kiss to her cheek, Franklin was out the door.

Catherine rang the doorman and asked to have another paper delivered to her apartment. She feverishly turned the pages until she came to the article she wanted. It read: "A special reception will be held tonight at the Grand View Gallery for renowned Spanish artist Alejandro Mendez."

Did she want to see him again? Did she dare see him again? A cacophony of emotions fought inside her.

Later that morning, Catherine called her husband's office. "Darling, there's an art exhibit I'd like to see this evening. Can we go?"

"Not tonight, I'm afraid. We're having dinner with one of the men up for partnership in my firm. We've had it on our schedule for weeks."

"Franklin, would you mind going by yourself just this once? It is only for one night, and I really would like to see this exhibit."

"Well, that depends. Do you trust me to evaluate

this young man without your opinion?" From his tone, Catherine knew he was smiling.

"Surely you know that I trust you, Franklin. How long have we been married? Twenty years? I have complete confidence in your judgment."

"All right dear, go and enjoy the show. I shouldn't be too late. I'll see you at home later tonight."

Catherine worked at a hectic pace that day, trying to keep her mind off her plans for the evening. Franklin went straight from work to dinner, so Catherine had time at home to take great pains with her dress and makeup. She looked at herself in the mirror. *I'm older, but not in a bad way. In fact, I think I look quite regal. He'll see what a prize he gave away.*

* * *

Catherine stepped into the gallery and immediately spotted Alejandro across the room. He was older, but still very handsome and distinguished. Her heart skipped a beat as she took in the striking young woman standing beside him.

Catherine accepted a glass of champagne and took her time looking at all the paintings in the gallery. They were impressive. She remembered the painting she still had packed away in storage –

maybe not as good as these, but oh so much more passionate.

Nerves and anxiety overtook her and she began to tremble. She was about to leave when she heard her name. She turned and saw Alejandro walking toward her.

"Catherine! Catherine Kingston. What a surprise!"

She responded with more frost in her voice than she had expected. "I'm Catherine Kingston Hughes now."

"Yes, I heard you had married. It's marvelous to see you, Catherine, after all these years. Come, meet my Rachel."

She allowed him to guide her to where Rachel was standing. "Catherine, this is my wife Rachel. Rachel, this is Catherine. Catherine's father made my studies possible and financed my first gallery."

Catherine stood in stunned silence and for a moment could not speak. *Wait, what did he say? What did Father have to do with Alejandro's gallery?* After taking a moment to recover, she put on her best smile and raised her glass. "Here's to old friends and your brilliant success."

Bewildered, confused, and hurt by what had just happened, Catherine felt the overwhelming need to leave. She exited quickly, leaving a note with

Alejandro's assistant asking him to meet with her. She wanted to meet with him privately and clear up what she surely misheard or misunderstood.

They met the next day at the coffee shop around the corner from the gallery. Catherine wasted no time with small talk. "What did you mean when you said my father financed your education and first gallery?"

"He made it possible for me with his money."

"Money? What money?"

Alejandro began filling in the blanks for Catherine. He told her how her father had offered him a grand sum in exchange for his vow to never contact her again. He told her that his money had paid for schooling and had allowed him to start his own gallery. He couldn't believe her father had kept the transaction a secret. After all, had she not married that Hughes man? After he finished talking, Catherine was destroyed.

"So you really took his money? What a coward you are. I thought you loved me! I waited for you. I wrote endless letters. Didn't you think you owed me some sort of explanation?"

"Catherine, I never even met your father. He sent his lawyer – your husband – and he was determined not to leave without my surrender. I did love you, Catherine. But we were young.

Sometimes money proves to be more practical than love. Twenty-five thousand dollars was too tempting to a young artist who craved training and a platform to showcase his art. I didn't want to admit I could be bought, but in the end I did take his money. I didn't resist. It was you or my art. You or my life."

"Franklin? *My* Franklin? He was the one who paid you off? That bastard!" Catherine slammed her coffee cup on the table. "Honestly, all of the men in my life are turning out to be bastards."

Alejandro sat with his head down and made no attempt to defend his actions. "I'm sorry, Catherine. If it's any consolation, I remember our affair with tenderness and no regrets."

Catherine stood up and looked at him with piercing eyes. She was tempted to throw her coffee in his face. Instead, without saying a word, she walked out of the cafe before he could see her tears.

When she arrived home, Catherine slammed the door and yelled for Franklin. He came from their bedroom in a cashmere robe, his glasses in one hand and a book in the other. "Hello, darling. How are you?"

"Why didn't you tell me that Father sent you to do his dirty work? What other lies are you hiding from me? How did I ever think you were a decent, honorable man?"

Franklin put his glasses down and tossed the book onto the divan. "I suppose you're referring to the Mendez affair. I saw his show advertised in the paper and assume that's where you went last night. Please, Catherine, it's not that big a deal." Putting his hands out, he continued, "Sit down with me so we can talk."

"I will not sit down."

Franklin continued. "Haven't you made an extraordinary career for yourself by running our business? Haven't we been happily married?"

"Don't you tell *me* how I feel. You and Father took away my one true chance at love, and I don't know if I can ever forgive you for that." Catherine paced the floor. "I want the whole story and I want it now. Every sordid little detail."

Franklin stood up and poured himself a scotch and soda. "You seem to have gotten the facts already. Who told you? Was it straight from the mouth of the morally bankrupt Spaniard himself?"

Catherine jerked the glass from his hands and threw it at the fireplace. "I want to hear it from *your* mouth! Stop dancing around it and tell me what happened."

Franklin was stunned. His red face was just inches from Catherine's. "So I'm the one who's lying now, am I? Just what did that little Spanish prick tell you? It was entirely your father's scheme, not mine. I was just the messenger. I was doing my job. Why all this anger now, and why direct it at me? Your father was the one who couldn't stand the idea that you'd marry someone without his blessing, and your faithless lover was the one that let you go."

Catherine fumed. "Don't you see that you're just as guilty as they are? You could have refused to be Father's henchman, but no, you ruined my life and then hid it from me for the last twenty years. You knew what you were doing from the start. And I suppose my father made it clear to you that you'd be the only man to get his blessing with me, right? So you carried out his plan – to perfection, I might add."

"Catherine, please. Your father did think it would be beneficial to all of us if I married you. But I didn't marry you because of that. I married you because you grew on me and I saw a brilliant future for us."

Catherine scoffed. "I *grew* on you? How convenient for me." She turned and pointed to the door. "I despise you, Franklin, and I can't believe I ever felt anything for you." Throwing his book at him, she yelled, "Get out!"

CHAPTER 10

In the hallway that connected the skilled nursing unit to the residences, Dr. Jeffery Neil was talking with Patsy. "Fannie Gerrick will need to stay at least two more weeks in skilled nursing so she can start physical therapy." He stopped abruptly when he saw his old high school friend coming through the doors of Balboa Shores.

"Casey Howell! Long time no see, buddy. What are you doing here?"

Casey kept his eyes fixed on Dr. Neil. "My dad is living here now. Is this one of your facilities?"

"I have a couple of patients here." Looking at Patsy, standing awkwardly with her eyes to the floor, Dr. Neil started to introduce her to Casey.

Casey interrupted in a clipped tone. "We've already met."

Conversation came to a halt. Neither Casey nor Patsy were smiling. Dr. Neil could feel the tension, and quickly returned to the topic at hand. "How is your dad, Casey?"

"Not good, I'm afraid. He's getting more senile. He seems to think he's twenty again."

"I'm sorry to hear he's getting worse. Regression happens with dementia, but then again, twenty's not such a bad age to be," said Dr. Neil, looking to

Patsy for agreement, but she was silent.

Casey continued. "I would tend to agree, but Dad keeps talking about getting married and he's keeping Carolyn and me in the dark."

"He's probably just lonely and wants some companionship," said Dr. Neil.

"Companionship is fine, but marriage is a different game altogether, and I can't be here twenty-four hours a day to watch over him."

"I can see you're concerned, Casey," said Dr. Neil. "The staff here is excellent at what they do. I don't think you have anything to worry about."

Looking directly at Patsy, Casey responded, "That's what I've been told."

Excusing herself, Patsy directed her remarks to Dr. Neil. "So good to see you, Dr. Neil. Mr. Howell has expressed his concerns to Ms. Jackson and we're keeping an eye on the situation. We're doing everything we can to keep Harry safe."

Patsy headed for the second floor, her head fuming. *Son of a biscuit, I think he's making far too much fuss about this. How could this angry man be related to sweet Harry?*

Waiting by the elevator, Patsy heard her second loud, angry voice of the morning. Fannie Louise Gerrick's husband, Peter, was fussing as he exited the skilled nursing wing.

"What does that doctor know anyhow? I'm her husband!" he shouted.

"Mr. Gerrick, what's wrong? Can I help?" asked Patsy.

"Help me? Nobody around this place helps me. Nobody listens to me. I'm just the husband, you know."

"Are you talking about the skilled nursing staff?"

"Yes." Mr. Gerrick was clearly agitated. "They won't let me get Fannie up to walk. She can do it, but they won't let her. I almost had her out of bed when they told me to stop and leave the room. They're spoiling her in there."

"She's still recuperating from a broken hip, Mr. Gerrick. We don't want her to fall again. Only trained staff are allowed to get her up and help her walk. They have special equipment in case she should start to fall. Dr. Neil told me she might be there for another two weeks."

"She's fine now. She can walk. I don't want her in a wheelchair."

Patsy asked gently, "Why don't you let the doctor decide if she needs a wheelchair or not?"

Peter raised his voice as he replied, "Those doctors don't know what's best for her. And in the meantime, I don't have a wife."

Getting on the elevator with Mr. Gerrick, Patsy

continued, "That's not true. You still have a wife. She'll be up and walking soon. But for now she needs to stay in the unit to get the help she needs."

"I help her more than anyone in there. And what about me? Who's going to take care of me?"

Patsy shook her head. "If you need help, Mr. Gerrick, all you need to do is ask for it. Any of the caregivers will be more than willing to help you."

"I can't afford your care. Fannie's daughters insist I pay for my room and board here, when Fannie has more than enough money to pay for everything." The elevator opened and Patsy watched him stomp away with an abrupt, dismissive wave of his hand. Peter Gerrick was more nasty and irrational than usual – a sign, Patsy suspected, of his worsening dementia.

Patsy turned and walked down the opposite hall. She was passing Beatrice's room when Beatrice opened the door. "Have you seen my mother?" Beatrice asked. "We were having tea and Mother was sitting in the rocker when she rocked over backwards and everything went flying. She was on the floor, the cup and saucer broken. Tea was everywhere. I went to get a towel and when I came back, she was gone."

Patsy knew that Beatrice's mother had been deceased for many years. "Bea, let me come in and see if I can find out what happened." Patsy walked into the studio, spotting the upright rocker and no sign of a teapot or teacups anywhere. However, the room was beyond messy – it was a horde. "Beatrice, sit down and try not to worry. I'll go see if she went downstairs." Patsy went to the nurse's office and told Nurse Jones about Beatrice's "missing" mother.

"When she gets confused, she can get a bit frantic," said the nurse. "I'll give her an Ativan and see if that calms her down."

"Why don't you let me take it to her? I'll sit with her a while and encourage her to work on her knitting. If she can get her mind off this episode and focus on something physical, maybe she'll calm down and won't need the pills."

Nurse Jones agreed. "Okay, but if she doesn't take the pill, be sure to bring it back. It's one of the drugs we need to keep a close eye on by logging it in and out. We've had problems in the past with a few dishonest staff members taking pills to residents and keeping them for their own use. I know you wouldn't do that, Patsy, but I need to follow protocol."

Patsy took the anti-anxiety pill and walked back toward Beatrice's room. Beatrice was standing in the door, bewilderment in her eyes.

"Beatrice, why don't you show me your latest knitting project?"

Beatrice's face immediately brightened. "Oh Patsy, I'd love to! I'm working on an afghan for the Christmas bazaar. I chose the red and green, but Catherine told me that those colors don't go together." Patsy followed Beatrice into her studio apartment, and Bea held up the partially completed afghan with one red stripe following each green stripe.

"It's beautiful, Beatrice. I think the colors are perfect. You better keep working on it if you want to finish by Christmas. Come, show me how it's done."

"I'll teach you anytime you want, Patsy. It's not hard, just time-consuming."

Patsy smiled. "I know it takes talent to produce something so beautiful. And I know I don't have the time nor the patience for it. However, I love watching you."

Patsy sat with Beatrice until she calmed down and became lost in her work, her missing mother no longer on her mind. Patsy left her, returned the Ativan to the med room, and gave it to Nurse Jones who dutifully logged it back in.

In the morning, Patsy brought the problem with Beatrice's messy room to the attention of the head housekeeper. She told Patsy that the stacks of boxes and other items made the room hard to clean, and that Beatrice would not let them remove anything without her approval. Patsy was dumbfounded. Traversing the room was difficult for agile adults, and could be downright dangerous for Beatrice. There were letters, junk mail, personal notes, newspapers, gum wrappers, cookie boxes, cotton swabs, books, string, rubber bands, menus, and unopened boxes from QVC and HSN. Patsy put in a call to Beatrice's children and requested a meeting.

The following day, Susan Jackson and Patsy met with Beatrice's oldest son, John. "Are you aware of the state of your mother's room?" Susan asked.

"Of course we are," John answered.

"Was this an ongoing problem before she came to Balboa Shores?"

John squirmed. "Yes," he admitted. "It was much worse at the house. It grew from the living room into the dining room, the bedrooms, the kitchen, and even the bathroom. Her bed was so buried she started sleeping in a recliner surrounded by piles of newspapers, magazines, and clothing. The kitchen was so cluttered, Mom couldn't cook or use her refrigerator. She landed in the hospital from a respiratory infection and malnutrition."

"Did you try to get help for her?" questioned Susan.

"Of course we did. After she left the hospital we took her to our home, rented a dumpster and cleaned the house out completely. Mom was very angry with us, but she promised to get organized. When she moved back in it just started all over. I think she was depressed. We didn't want her to fall and break a hip, and we thought she would be safer here."

Susan's face made it clear that she was unsympathetic. "It should have been disclosed before your mom was accepted for residency. We don't have the staff to clean out all the clutter, and it's spreading like a weed patch."

John slumped in his chair and put his hands over his eyes. At last he looked at Susan. "What else can be done?"

"We can contract for a professional organizer to help your mother. You will need to pay her and there will be extra care points for us to monitor the situation. Or, you can try to keep it under control yourself."

"We've already tried and failed, so I guess we'll have to go with your suggestion."

"I appreciate that. By the end of the week, the room needs to be cleaned out and kept clear, or you might have to find another facility for Beatrice."

Beatrice's children came out in full force and cleaned out the studio. Everything seemed to go well for a while.

CHAPTER 11
CATHERINE KINGSTON HUGHES
NEW YORK, SUMMER 1975

After the divorce, Catherine worked long hours and rambled around in her large penthouse. She took little part in social affairs. She did, however, go out to dinner on occasion with business acquaintances. Most of these dinners would start with, "What do you hear from Franklin?"

"I don't," she would reply stiffly.

"We know he would like to talk to you. He still cares for you, you know. You were such a successful couple. We all hope you get back together." The constant talk of reconciliation gave her a picture of where her friends' true loyalties lay. Catherine refused all further invitations.

* * *

She started painting again, and spent a great deal of her time alone in her apartment working on canvas after canvas, experimenting with different styles and mediums. She began showing up late to the office and missing important business meetings. At first her staff thought she was legitimately detained, but as this happened more frequently, they moved from annoyed to worried. Catherine became obsessed with her artwork at the expense of her company. Her concentration became erratic; her leadership unfocused. Without Catherine's scrupulous supervision, an inept manager within the company allowed several dubious business deals to be made.

Tom Brown, CFO of Apex, was becoming worried about the health of the company and thought that Catherine might be headed for a mental breakdown. After she was a no-show at the annual shareholders meeting, he tried to telephone her and grew concerned when she didn't answer. Tom mentioned to his secretary as he left the office, "She's become so reclusive and isolated; she could be ill or have fallen or be dead and no one would know for days. I'm going over there to see what's going on."

After unsuccessfully buzzing the penthouse, Tom rang the manager and explained the situation. "I might need you to unlock her door. We haven't been able to raise her by phone and she didn't answer when I called up just now." The manager accompanied Tom to the penthouse and, after repeatedly knocking, pulled out his keyring and opened the door.

Inside, Tom found the apartment littered with

dirty dishes, paint pots, newspapers, and scattered clothes. "Catherine, it's Tom Brown. Are you here? Catherine? Are you okay?"

Catherine sat outside on the terrace with her easel, staring at the blank canvas in front of her. She was surrounded by stacks of paintings – some quite good, some primitive, others just blobs of paint randomly smeared over the surface. Her appearance was disheveled, and her naturally thin frame was now gaunt. She took no notice of Tom who, worried and now frightened, called the family doctor.

"Doctor Erck, I think you'd better come over here. Catherine is in bad shape. She's not responding but she's not unconscious. I don't know how to describe it ... yes, she's breathing, but she's not responding to anything I say. It's almost like she's hypnotized or something. I think you should see for yourself. I don't want to take her to the hospital if it's not necessary."

When the doctor arrived, it became quickly apparent to him that Catherine was in a fugue state. He called an ambulance and had her taken to the hospital. The diagnosis was senior dementia and catatonic depression.

Catherine spent several months in a private psychiatric hospital, after which Tom took over as

CEO of Apex. With Franklin's assistance, he attained conservatorship over Catherine's affairs. Balboa Shores was considered one of the best long-term care facilities for seniors with memory problems and dementia, and it was far enough away that she could not cause a problem. There they would keep a careful eye on Catherine's personal hygiene, health, and safety.

CHAPTER 12

Buckets of black paint and seniors with dementia. *Probably not the best combination*, Patsy thought, but she was intent on having the residents make black spiders on the windows of the Activities Room for Halloween.

Miss Millie was reluctant to get her hand painted black. "It's too messy, Patsy. What if I get it in my hair?"

"We'll be careful. I'll put the paint on your palm and four fingers, but not your thumb." She took the paint brush and painted Miss Millie's hand black. "Now put your hand to the window and press against it." Patsy held Miss Millie's hand on the window to help out. "Great. Now let's do the other hand and go the other direction to make four more legs." Four legs stuck out on each side of a black palm-shaped blob. "Great job, Miss Millie. Now why don't you go wash your hands in the sink while I put some googly eyes on the spider."

Patsy was pleased that the other residents seemed excited to make their own spiders on the windows. Patsy focused her attention on helping them one at a time. After the first four residents finished, she looked around the room.

Instead of washing her hands, Maisie had

smeared the black paint all over her face. Delbert had used his fingers to paint the game table. Patsy, spotting some black smears on the couch, was suspicious that Catherine had used it to wipe her hands clean. She sighed and said, "I think we have the perfect number of spiders on the windows. Let's get everyone cleaned up and maybe start a game of dominoes." The domino game was a success and Patsy breathed a sigh of relief.

Later that evening, Patsy sipped a glass of Chardonnay at her own dining table while planning a Halloween-themed activity for the residents. As she filled several small Halloween baskets with spider rings, small rubber rats, and wrapped candies, she decided to explain the activity tomorrow after the weekly memory games.

Patsy addressed the residents the next morning. "It's a fun and simple game – kind of like playing telephone, but instead of passing a message around, we'll secretly pass treats to each other. See these ten baskets filled with goodies? I'm going to hang them on your doorknobs, but you won't know who's getting one until you see it. When the basket lands on your doorknob, you get to take one treat out of the basket and keep it for yourself." Patsy glanced around the room, looking for a glimmer of understanding or recognition. She continued.

"Each basket also has several slips of paper inside them that say I'VE BEEN BOOED! After you take your treat, take one of the slips of paper out of the basket and tape it to your front door so that everyone will know that you've had your turn. The last step is the fun part – you get to hang the basket on someone else's door. You want to pick someone who hasn't been "booed" yet, so don't leave the basket if you see a sign on their door. Does everyone understand?" Heads nodded all around.

After all her preparation, Patsy might as well have asked the residents to file each other's income taxes. No one understood, and no one followed through. Even with encouragement from the caregivers, the residents failed to get the idea. Catherine complained that some crude person left a basket of offensive objects at her door. Maisie took her basket to dinner and passed out the entire contents. Beatrice ended up with five of the ten baskets in her room (to which Patsy gently suggested that she donate some baskets back to the next bingo auction). She also rethought the Secret Santa idea that had been percolating in her head and quickly ditched it.

* * *

Bingo was big business at Balboa Shores. It was played several times a week and each time Bingo Bucks were handed out to the winners. Bingo Bucks were paper bills that the winners could spend at the monthly bingo auction. Up for auction this afternoon was an assortment of pencils, pens, note cards, toiletries, knick knacks, food, and small electrical items. Peter Gerrick always saved his Bingo Bucks for at least two months and then came to the auction ready to win against anyone and everyone.

Patsy thought the Halloween decorations and colorful fall leaves gave the auction a festive air. The auctioneer began. "The first item up for bid is a day-glow flashlight. We'll start the bidding at three hundred."

Maisie, waving her Bingo Bucks in the air, bid three hundred.

"Four hundred," responded Peter.

"Five hundred," said Maisie.

"One thousand," countered Peter.

"Going once at one thousand," said the auctioneer, looking around at the other residents. "Going twice." Silence. "Sold to Mr. Gerrick for one thousand dollars." The auctioneer pounded his gavel. "Up next is a boxed set of all-occasion cards. Who will give me two hundred dollars?"

Miss Millie shouted, "Two hundred!"

"Do I hear three hundred?" No one bid against Miss Millie, who smiled as the auctioneer handed her the box of cards.

Peter bid against Beatrice for a stuffed black cat and won. He grinned his triumphant grin. "Perfect for my grandson's birthday."

The next item was a set of lace doilies. Olga bid three hundred. Peter bid five hundred.

Patsy interrupted. "Peter, you can't bid yet. You're only allowed two items until everyone else has had a chance." Peter was always pushing the rules.

"Besides," Olga said, "what do you want with doilies? You don't really want them. You just don't want me to have them."

Peter stood up as he responded, "I do want them! I want to give them to my daughter for Christmas."

"You know Fannie's been wanting doilies for her tables. I'm going to get them for her," finished Olga, sticking her tongue out at Peter.

Once again, Patsy found herself intervening. "Peter, the rule is only two buys before everyone has had a chance. So Olga, it's your bid."

"She can have 'em," Peter snapped. "She better not give them to Fannie, though. They're just dust catchers and I don't want them cluttering up my apartment."

"Let's see what we have here," said the auctioneer, holding the next item in the air. "These will keep someone warm and toasty tonight. Let's start the bidding at five hundred."

Olga spoke up. "Five hundred."

"Six hundred," said Peter.

"Delbert hasn't had a chance to bid yet," said Patsy. "Do you want to bid on these, Delbert?" The auction was noisy and confusing for Delbert, who would often sit the whole time with his Bingo Bucks in his hand and not bid unless prompted.

"What are they?"

"They're slipper socks. You need to bid seven hundred if you want them."

Delbert scratched his head. "Well, I don't rightly know. Are they slippers or are they socks?"

"They're both. You wear them instead of slippers and you can wear them to bed, too," Patsy said.

"Nah, I don't think I want them. My socks do just fine."

"Then they're mine," smiled Peter.

CHAPTER 13
SARAH ELIZABETH OWEN
WISCONSIN, SUMMER 1913

At Balboa Shores, ninety-year-old Sarah Elizabeth Owen was sitting in her room reading her Bible when she felt her chair tip backwards and her Bible tumbled to the floor. It was her next-door neighbor, Catherine. Sarah put her hands to her heart. "Oh Catherine, you frightened me so. I didn't hear you come in."

"I knocked," Catherine lied as she pushed Sarah's chair upright and sat down on the foot stool in front of her. "I need my hair braided." Catherine liked her hair in one thick braid down her back. Once Catherine found Sarah was willing to take time to braid her hair, she took liberal advantage of Sarah's kindness.

Catherine led Sarah around like a child, even though she was about twenty years younger than her quiet friend. Catherine's demanding personality and voice often grated on Sarah, much like a razor blade, hard and sharp. But Sarah knew her bohemian crony didn't have many friends, and Sarah had spent her life being a friend to the friendless.

When Sarah finished braiding, Catherine left

without as much as a thank you. Sarah leaned her chair back and closed her weary eyes. In her mind's eye she saw herself as a young girl wearing a plain yoked dress, her hair tied back with a blue ribbon, laughing as she chased a young boy over the large grassy expanse of an old hotel in Waukesha, Wisconsin.

* * *

Holding a finger to his lips, the boy spoke. "Sarah, Sarah, shhhh. You have to sneak up very quietly and close the top of the hollyhock if you want to trap the bees. Laughing will scare them away." Sarah and her friend Seth were competing to see who could trap the most bees and then let them go.

They had both grown up as part of a religious commune. An old hotel had been sectioned off, giving each family a small set of rooms, and renamed the Fountain House. Here, each person worked for the good of all.

At age ten, Sarah and Seth had a relatively normal childhood, chasing bees and helping out with the occasional job here and there. By age sixteen, however, both had been working in the community garden every day after school. They worked side by side, helping each other by sharing their chores. After pulling Seth's weeds, they knelt to plant Sarah's carrot seeds. She began to poke a hole in the dirt with her finger.

"What assignment do you want next?" They were now at the age of consent, and would have some say as to where they would work next.

Seth stopped and looked at her. "I suppose I want to work on the farm, with the livestock, not so much in the fields though. What about you?"

"I think it's the kitchen for me, but I can't see myself cooking for the rest of my life. I want to do something important, something to really help people."

"Don't you think living and working here is important and helpful?"

"Sure I do," she said as she went to get the water hose. "Never mind. I was just thinking out loud." Seth sat back on his heels, watching her. She smiled at him and started to water the newly planted carrot seeds.

She wondered if he knew that the Fellowship thought they would make a good couple. From the talk it seemed most considered them already betrothed. *Maybe that's what the Fellowship wants,* thought Sarah, *but I'm not so sure I want to settle down and work the earth for Jesus' sake.* What good did that do Jesus? Well, they did support missionaries with money made from the sale of excess produce, but Sarah couldn't think of much else that was good about it.

True to course, Sarah began working in the kitchen where, for two years, she cooked and served meals to the Fellowship. One evening at dinner, the Deacon called Sarah over to his table.

"Sarah, could we have a different bowl of gravy, please? This one seems to be a bit lumpy."

"Yes, Deacon, right away."

"I know the lumps are not your fault, Sarah, but we must all do our best for the Lord, even if it's only making gravy." Sarah removed the offending gravy bowl and hurried back with a replacement.

"Deacon, I'm sorry about the gravy. Could I speak with you after dinner, in private?"

"Of course, my dear. I'll be in my office and I'd be more than happy to see you. Nothing wrong, I hope?" Sarah, not wanting to share in front of so many people, shook her head and began clearing away the dishes from the next table to make way for dessert.

She was nervous as she rapped softly on the Deacon's office door. When there was no response she took a deep breath and knocked again, louder. The Deacon opened the door. "Come in, come in. I was just having a moment of prayer to provide direction and wisdom. Now, what is bothering you, Sarah?"

"Deacon, I would like to leave the kitchen and work in the infirmary."

"I see." The Deacon took off his glasses and placed them onto the table next to him. "I'm not sure your parents would approve, Sarah. It's hard work, very hard, and you're not trained for it. I'm not sure you're strong enough for such heavy work."

Disappointed, Sarah crossed her arms and turned her back to him for a moment. When she turned back to face the Deacon, she planted her hands on the desk firmly in front of him. Leaning forward, she began again. "And how will I get trained if I never get the chance to try? There are people dying daily from this epidemic. It's the Spanish flu, for God's sake! The infirmary doesn't have enough people to help, and I can't just keep serving food when I would be of more help to the sisters."

The Deacon was surprised by this uncharacteristic outburst coming from the sweet, quiet Sarah. He promised to talk with her parents about her request. "I'm eighteen, no longer a child. I think I can decide for myself where I can do the most good."

The next Sunday, Sarah began her work in the

infirmary. Tired and pale from the long, hard hours – made harder by so few recovering patients – an exhausted Sarah sat in the Sunday evening service. The sermon featured missionaries, home on furlough from India, speaking about their work. They spoke of their lives and the desperate need for more workers. *If people are suffering like this in the United States, how much worse must it be in India?*

Her thoughts were confirmed when the missionaries told the fellowship that India was one of the hardest hit countries in this worldwide scourge that was now known as the Great Flu Epidemic of 1918. Sarah was sure India was her destiny, and she was determined to go there as soon as possible.

CHAPTER 14
NOVEMBER

It had taken more than one invitation from Brenda Brownlee for Patsy to join the girls for a night out dancing, but now she was glad she'd said yes. The music at Denim and Diamonds tonight was good and loud. Everyone seemed to know Brenda. She was laughing, dancing, and downing more than a few beers. Brenda introduced Patsy to everyone who stopped by their table. Patsy wore new jeans, new boots, and more makeup than usual. She was actually enjoying herself. Most of the men were well-behaved and friendly.

Patsy noticed a man sitting alone in the corner of the room, drinking, his cowboy hat tipped low over his eyes. He stood up and approached their table with a well-practiced swagger. He was tall, muscular, and wore a surely smirk. His eyes had been on her all evening. He walked right up to Patsy.

"Little lady, I think it's time you and I take a swing around the dance floor." A slow number was playing.

Patsy stopped smiling. "No, I don't think so. But thank you for asking." She turned her head and hoped he'd take it as a sign that the conversation was over.

She gave the cowboy too much credit. Taking her hand and pulling her up from her chair, he slurred, "I don't take no for an answer. Let me show you how a real cowboy does it."

Not wanting to make a scene, she let herself be led to the dance floor. The cowboy held her way too tight, and his hands wandered down over the back of her jeans and pressed her closer. She could smell whiskey on his breath. She kept her head turned away, waiting for the song to end.

When the music finally stopped, she left him standing on the dance floor and made her way to the ladies' room. She was just about to enter when a hand grabbed her wrist.

"Now missy, that's not a very polite way to thank a gentleman for a dance," the whiskey-soaked cowboy rasped. Patsy tried to jerk away, but he had a tight hold on her arm.

"I think the lady made it quite clear," said a voice from behind her. Patsy glanced up to see Casey Howell standing next to her, breaking the grip the man had on Patsy's arm. "Why don't you go back to your table and have some coffee. Maybe if you sober up and mind your manners, the ladies will find you slightly more tolerable."

"Mind your own business," growled the man as

he swung his fist at Casey. Casey blocked the drunken punch, then twisted the man's arm behind his back, holding it until they reached the man's table. Casey pushed him down in a chair.

The club manager spotted the skirmish and came over. "Is there a problem, Casey?"

"It's Rooney again. He's being obnoxious and aggressive with a friend of mine."

The manager frowned. "Rooney, I've told you before not to start anything when you come in here. I've had enough and you've clearly had more than enough. I'm cutting you off. You'd do best to get out of here now and go home to that pretty wife of yours." The manager had his bouncer escort Rooney out of the club.

When Patsy came out of the ladies room, she ran into Casey. "I know you were trying to help, but I can handle myself, Mr. Howell."

"Well, you're very welcome," offered Casey. "From where I was standing, it didn't look like you were handling it very well at all."

"I handled it by walking away, not with bullying."

"And what would you have done if he was still here waiting for you when you came out of the bathroom? Rooney causes problems whenever he comes here and drinks, which is pretty much all the time."

"Seeing that this is my first time here, I didn't know that. You, however, seem to know your way around here quite well. Doesn't your wife object to you spending time in bars?"

"I don't have a wife. I'm not married. I come here for a beer with my crew after work a few times a week. I try to mind my own business. I was only trying to help."

"I'm sorry, I guess I'm a little confused. First you accuse me of being a gold digger and then you come to my rescue. I don't think many gold diggers come to cowboy bars, but then again what do I know?"

Casey turned to Brenda. "Brenda, tell your friend she's got a point there. I'll consider it." And with that, Casey walked out of Denim and Diamonds.

Patsy was exasperated. "Brenda, how do you know him?"

"Calm down, Patsy. Casey is a regular here. I bartend here two nights a week and he's a really decent guy. I'm surprised you didn't thank him for taking care of Rooney for you."

Patsy sighed. "Casey's father is a resident at Balboa Shores. He thinks that I flirt with his father and intend to marry him for his money. If you'd had to put up with what I've put up with from him, you might not be so enamored with Casey Howell."

Brenda cut her short. "But you must admit, he saved your ass just now."

"Yeah, you've got a point there."

"Where did you get the idea he was married?"

"He talked about someone named Carolyn when he made his complaint at work."

"Carolyn's his sister, Patsy. He's not married. So how about cutting him some slack?"

Oh, thought Patsy. "Like he said, I'll think about it. Now why don't we get something to eat? I'm starving."

CHAPTER 15
SARAH ELIZABETH OWEN
INDIA, FALL 1920

Sarah awoke from her nap to the chimes that announced dinner was ready at Balboa Shores. The sound reminded Sarah of the chimes she had first heard on the ocean liner, on her trip to India. First a high, and then a lower ding dong (except at Balboa Shores no one announced "First call for dinner!"). Her thoughts took her back to the year she boarded the ship, and to her foolish actions. She still felt the shame ...

A twenty-year-old Sarah set sail to India on the O&P Steamship line. Thirty-five dollars bought her the twelve-day ticket in second class, where meals were served family-style. Dinner was usually a very good beef or lamb stew, vegetables, and homemade bread. Sarah had gotten to know her table mates a bit and felt comfortable in their presence. After dinner, she would go out on deck and listen to the beautiful music drifting down from the first class dining room. The moon hit the tops of the waves, giving the water a fairy-like twinkle under a sky filled with millions of stars. Having never left the United States before, Sarah was excited and felt as though she was traveling in the lap of luxury.

After a week, the ship stopped in London to board new passengers. Sarah leaned over the rail, watching the newcomers arrive. First class passengers were allowed on first. She watched them stroll up the gangplank, looking so sophisticated, wearing large plumed hats, velvet coats, and dainty slippers. One of the young men looked her in the eye and smiled as he doffed his hat to her. Sarah's cheeks burned but she smiled, and then quickly averted her eyes.

Half an hour later, she heard the two prolonged blasts from the ship's whistle and covered her ears. *Now I'm really on my way to India,* she thought, as the ship moved slowly out of port.

That evening she went out on deck as usual, and got lost in the spray and the smell of the sea. A voice from above startled her. "Good evening, miss." Turning around and looking up, Sarah saw the young man who had smiled at her earlier, looking even more handsome in his evening tuxedo. She had thought he must be English, but his voice revealed him to be American.

Holding a cigarette casually in one hand, he asked, "May I come down and introduce myself?"

"If you'd like," Sarah replied softly.

"Oh, yes, I'd like that very much." He came down the stairs and jumped over the chain blocking the way.

After taking a last puff on his cigarette, he put it out and extended his hand. "I'm Jason Hightower. How do you do?"

Sarah offered her hand. "Very well, thank you. I'm Sarah Owen. Are you on your way to India as well?" The aroma he exuded was acrid and sweet. Sarah wondered if he was wearing perfume. *In all my life, I've never met a man wearing perfume.*

"No, I'm going to Port Said to visit my grandfather for a few weeks." He looked her up and down before asking, "What on earth could possibly be in India for a girl like you?"

"I'm going to Allahabad as a missionary."

"Allahabad? Never heard of it. Must be very remote."

"Not at all," she said. "It's not far from Delhi."

"Northwest India, where the Hindus and Muslims are always fighting? I bet they'll forget about fighting and fall at your feet when they see your golden hair and beautiful blue eyes," he said as he twirled a strand of her hair and moved closer.

Sarah backed up. "Is your grandfather ill? This is an awfully long trip just for a visit."

"No, he's in the British Foreign Office that oversees the safety of the Canal. He wants me to experience military life before I start Cambridge."

"Cambridge, Massachusetts?" Sarah blurted out.

Jason laughed. "No, not that Cambridge. The one in England. I'm going to school there. My grandfather is hoping to influence me to carry on the military family tradition. That's not likely, though, I can assure you."

Sarah lowered her head in embarrassment. Jason ducked down to look in her eyes. "Homesick already?" he inquired.

"No, I'm just excited. I never thought I would actually be going to India, and the trip is a little overwhelming."

"You won't stay long, I predict. I've heard India is dry and dirty and the food is horrid."

"I'm not going for the food. I'm going to feed the hungry, help the sick and bring them the knowledge of the love of God."

"Mighty high ideals for such a beautiful young lady. A beautiful woman such as yourself really should be dancing." He pulled her close and began to move, the music trickling down softly from upstairs. Sarah stiffened. Dancing was not allowed in her Fellowship and she didn't know how.

"It was nice meeting you, Mr. Hightower, but it's late and I'm getting cold." Shivering, Sarah tried to step around him. Jason stopped her, took off his coat, and put it around her shoulders. *How gentlemanly,* thought Sarah.

"Let me walk you back to your cabin."

Sarah smiled and nodded. They walked down the long hallway in companionable silence. When she opened her door, Jason shoved her in and quickly locked the door behind him. He started to kiss Sarah and she turned her head away. He grabbed her head and twisted her arm behind her back, smashing his mouth onto hers, his tongue thrust into her mouth. She tried to scream, but he covered her mouth as he forced her down on the bed. Sarah tried to push him off, but was no match for him as he lifted her skirt and ripped at her undergarments.

Sarah's panic shifted into pain as she felt him penetrate her. Her eyes were wide and searching for rescue, but none came. She endured this nightmare by letting her mind go blank until, after what seemed like hours of agony, Jason finally rolled off her, gasping for breath. Sarah gathered her skirt and curled up in the corner of the bed.

"Get out," she sobbed. "Get out."

He stood, bowed, and sneered, "As you wish, Sarah Owen." And he was gone.

Sarah's cabin creaked and rolled on the rough sea through the night and into the next day. She stayed curled up in her bed, feeling sick, scared, and ashamed. She didn't know if she could stand nine and a half more days of this. People had warned her that the Mediterranean around Gibraltar could be rough, but they didn't tell her she would be so sick that she'd want to die. Her body was sore, her mind so filled with fear and guilt. She did not see how she could ever face the world again. She avoided looking in the mirror, afraid it would show a common trollop. *Surely the missionaries won't want me now,* she thought. The Fellowship had preached that premarital sex was only slightly below murder. Withdrawing, she was determined to stay in her cabin for the remainder of the trip.

After missing Sarah at several meals, an Indian woman who shared her table paid a visit to her cabin. Opening the door just a crack, Sarah was careful not to reveal what had happened to her. Instead, she told the woman she had been seasick and couldn't abide the look or smell of the ship's food.

"My sweet girl, you need to eat." The woman brought Sarah some tea, toast, and a small cup of broth. "You'll never get feeling better if you stay down here all day. You need some fresh air." Sarah resisted, not eager to have even a chance sighting of Jason. She only consented on the day the ship was to traverse the Suez Canal, knowing that Jason would already have left the ship.

The woman led Sarah outside and ordered her husband to giver her his seat. Sarah had to admit that the fresh air felt wonderful. It proved also to be a good antidote for her poor appetite. Passing through the locks was interesting, but the view of so much concrete soon became tedious. *What am I doing going so far away from the safety of home?* If she couldn't even trust her own judgment, how could she expect to be effective as a missionary?

The last few days of the journey, the ship sailed directly into the oppressive heat of the Indian Ocean. Sarah spent most of her time on the deck, watching gulls circle the ship as they looked for scraps of food thrown from the galley below. Sarah was happy the ocean voyage was almost at an end. She knew she would be met by someone from the mission, and she worried that it might be Brother Fordham. She had met Brother Fordham the night he and his wife spoke at the Fellowship. The possibility of traveling alone with a man filled her with anxiety and made her heart race wildly. Could she trust herself to be safe with any man ever again?

Brother Fordham did meet her and they continued the trip by rail from Bombay to Allahabad. The trip was miserable, dirty, dusty, and crowded.

Brother Fordham did not seem to be bothered by any of these circumstances. As Sarah sat meekly in her seat, he was talkative and pointed out different castes of people, places and customs as they traveled along.

They arrived late in Allahabad and, because the mission had no money for rooms, they continued on about seven miles by ox cart to the mission station. Physically and mentally exhausted, Sarah fell into her small bed in the wee hours of the morning.

CHAPTER 16

Warm, delicious smells drifted down the hall as Catherine, holding Sarah by the hand, rushed toward the dining room. "Be careful, Sarah. I don't want you to trip and fall, but you need to walk faster." Sarah was struggling to keep up. She looked up at Catherine with sweet gentle eyes and quickened her steps.

Catherine's rush to lunch had a purpose – she was jockeying to get the large table in the middle of the dining room before it filled up. The two women sat together at every meal. Catherine always admonished Sarah during mealtimes – to keep her napkin on her lap, or cut her meat into smaller pieces. Their table companions considered Catherine's treatment overbearing, and it bothered everyone that Sarah allowed Catherine to bully her. Not wanting to be rude or embarrass Sarah, the others tried their best to ignore Catherine until she became so annoying that they tried to fill up the table before the two arrived.

When the two did arrive first, the other residents avoided the table, leaving Sarah and Catherine all alone at the large middle table. Even sitting with Delbert, who sometimes forgot to put in his dentures, and his dog, who scooted around the table eating crumbs and licking toes, was preferable to dining with the domineering Catherine. Finding themselves the only two at the table didn't seem to bother Sarah, and Catherine was happy to be sitting at the "main table" even if the others chose to sit elsewhere.

"The same food every week," complained Catherine. "Don't you get tired of it, Sarah?"

"I'm grateful to have meals provided for me. The portions are so large, though. I hate to see so much good go to waste."

Catherine took Sarah's napkin and placed it on her lap. "Don't whine, Sarah. It sounds like you don't appreciate the efforts the cooks have made."

"I'm sorry, Catherine. I am grateful. I just wish I could share it with others who don't have what we do."

"Nonsense. Our nation is the most generous one on earth. We feed the world."

Delbert looked over at Sarah from his table, smiled his sweet smile, and mouthed *hello*. Sarah nodded in recognition of his greeting.

"Don't you two make a pair," sneered Catherine. "He can't hear and you can't speak above a whisper, too shy and timid to speak to each other. Why do you sit with him hour after hour in those two chairs in the Great Room in total silence? You blush like teenagers over a silly smile and a nod. I don't know why you want the attention of an old hayseed from the sticks of Kentucky."

"Catherine, you shouldn't talk about Delbert like that. It must be lonely living in a world where you don't hear well. I don't seek out his attention. I enjoy sitting quietly and it seems the friendly thing to do."

"Well, if you ask me, he wants a little more of you than just your attention."

"Neither of us has ever been married, and I think that gives us a mutual understanding of each other."

"Does that understanding include the flowers he picks for you out of the garden?"

"I grew up on a farm and he knows I enjoy simple things, like hollyhocks, so he brings me one every once in a while. He's a very kind and gentle man, a gentleman. He's just easy to be around."

"Well, let me tell you, Sarah. He doesn't seem like any gentleman I've ever known. Gentlemen are far more sophisticated, and true gentlemen are few and far between. Oh lord, here he comes now."

Delbert stopped at their table on his way out. "Hello Sarah, Catherine. Did you enjoy your dinner this evening?"

"Dinner was lovely, Delbert," Sarah whispered.

He bent over and cupped his ear. "What's that, Sarah?"

Sarah cleared her throat and spoke a little louder. "I said, dinner was very good, thank you."

"There's goin' to be music in the Great Room after dinner. Jack and I will be there." He nodded, winked, and walked away, leaning on his walker and whistling for Jack to follow.

After dinner, Catherine went with Sarah to the Great Room and sat down across the room from Delbert. The music was performed by a college student who played classical pieces first, and then asked if there were any requests. Catherine thought the requests were pedestrian, and soon decided to leave and go back to her room. Sarah was also tired, not of the music, just plain bone tired. She left with Catherine, anxious to lay her head down on her pillow.

CHAPTER 17
SARAH ELIZABETH OWEN
INDIA, SPRING 1925

Sarah had been forever changed by the rape aboard the steamship. The feeling that she had brought it on herself by dipping her toes in the ocean of worldly temptations tortured her. She had no one to console or comfort her, no one to tell her she was merely the innocent victim of a male raised by a class so privileged and so callous that the consequences of his actions no longer held any meaning. She prayed daily, begging forgiveness for her soiled body and unworthy soul. She had confessed her sin to God and no one else would ever know. She was determined to be the most dedicated and godly missionary India had ever seen.

She longed for the simple comfort and safety of family. How long before she would get a furlough? Eight, nine, ten years? Of course she received letters, but they were terribly out of date. She never disclosed any hint of her melancholy in her responses. She tried to give her family an uplifting, if not entirely accurate, picture of her life.

Dear Momma and Papa,

Love to you all. I think about you and pray for you every day. I hope you do the same for me. I'll try to tell you a little about my life here in far off India.

Every morning we rise at four o'clock for a prayer service before our chato-bazi, a small breakfast of tea and fruit. Then I go to the crowded bazaar to pass out religious tracts which have been translated into Hindi and Urdu. A girl named Aja has been assigned to me until I am comfortable with the language. I get little instruction, and must pick it up as I can.

Most mornings there are natives outside their huts watching as I pass. Aja tells me they aren't used to seeing young women who have blue eyes and light skin and hair. One morning a family invited me in to eat with them. I had, of course, already had my chato-bazi, but I was happy to be welcomed into a Hindu home and they seemed excited and happy that I accepted. The invitation did not extend to Aja as she was, in their eyes, my servant. Aja told me to go ahead and not worry about her. She would stay outside by the door.

As I was about to dip my fingers (they don't use forks and spoons here) into warm millet porridge (sweetened with coconut milk and mango), Aja cautioned me from the doorway not to use my left hand. The left hand is used only to wipe yourself and perform other dirty chores. I must admit, being left-handed, I am having some trouble adjusting to that custom. She also reminded me that it was getting late and we needed to be at the bazaar soon. How good Aja is. I would be constantly late and embarrassed if not for her.

In the afternoon I take a short rest to recuperate from the intense heat. I read scripture or just close my eyes and try to picture all of you. Then I work in the mission's school, or in the infirmary, or study Hindi.

In the evening we have a church meeting where a few of the natives attend. We tell them about the mission's many services, and then they are told about the plan of salvation in its simplest form. The best part is the singing. They don't understand the words, but much to the dismay of the missionaries, they love the sound of the music and insist on happily dancing and making strange noises as they sing along. If we did this at home, we would be prayed for, to turn from our worldly ways!

I have seen some of the most fascinating and beautiful animals here – elephants (which I think rather odd-looking with their short triangular ears), tigers, cobras, and Indian peacocks.

How is Margaret doing in her new teaching position? I suppose it is hard for her, the old sleepy head, to get up and be at the school house early enough to clean and prepare for her students.

Momma and Papa, I love you both and pray that you don't worry about me. I'm trying to fulfill God's plan for me although I feel at times totally inadequate. Tell everyone at Fountain House that I am doing well, and to pray for me and the lost souls here in India.

Your loving daughter,
Sarah Elizabeth

CHAPTER 18
DELBERT FLOWERS
KENTUCKY, 1970

Delbert, wearing his ever-present bib overalls, stopped Patsy in the hallway and smiled at her. "I'm going to get my hair clipped," he stated.

"Going to make yourself beautiful for Thanksgiving?" joked Patsy as she stooped down to pet Delbert's service dog, Jack.

"My sister always clipped it for me, but now I get clipped twice," said Delbert.

"Twice? Why twice?" asked Patsy.

"I get clipped once in my hair and once in my wallet," he chuckled.

It was always fun to talk with good-natured Delbert. He came to Balboa Shores the same year as Sarah. He came not because of the memory problems that were now surfacing, but because he had no practice at living on his own. For the first several months after arriving, Delbert was so timid he only left his room for meals. The rest of the time he spent fascinated by this new contraption called television.

* * *

Delbert's Kentucky family consisted of two boys and two girls. Delbert was the youngest. His older brother was killed in World War II. One sister, Lavinia, had married and moved to Illinois. Lavada, Lavinia's twin sister (and a true spinster if ever there was one) lived with lifelong bachelor Delbert in the same home where they were both born.

In spite of his shy nature, Delbert always had a smile on his face. He never uttered an unkind word, never had an enemy, and never held a steady job. It wasn't that he was lazy, just easy-going and challenged since childhood by near deafness.

Lavada, on the other hand, was made from piss and vinegar and rarely displayed a smile. It was common knowledge that she never got over being the wallflower twin. She took care of her little brother, Delbert, and worked as a clerk at the local dime store. She was an honest and faithful employee, but the young people of town complained that she scolded them for touching things in the store, and incorrectly counted out their change.

Lavada walked the two-mile trip to town every day until the day the store closed its doors for good. When she applied for unemployment compensation, they told her she had to prove that she was looking for work in order to receive her monthly check. So, in her mid-seventies, she would walk to town and go to the few small shops asking if they needed help, knowing they would not. They would sign the necessary form while teasing her.

"Wouldn't it be easier if you just found a man to marry and take care of you?"

To which she would reply, in total seriousness, "Who would marry me and take Delbert to boot?"

Home was at the very end of County Road 123. Their property backed up to the woods, and a dirt road connected it to the county road. There weren't any sidewalks and neighbors were few. Ready to walk to town, Lavada carefully negotiated the rickety front steps. At the bottom, she turned to Delbert, who was sitting in his rocking chair on the porch, and said, "Roy called. He has a few odds and ends he needs done at his farm. Said he'll pay you. Are you gonna sit there all day whittling, or do you think you could help him out today?"

"I'm just about done with this," said Delbert, laying down his whittling and picking up an old fishing pole and a can of night-crawlers. "I was gonna go fishing, but it's a mite late for them to be bitin'. I'll walk on over and help Roy and go fishing later t'night." Delbert's odd jobs were a small financial help.

Coldale Bankers had been trying to get the siblings to sell their property for the last year. They wanted to build something called a strip mall, but Delbert and Lavada had no interest in selling their childhood home. The old house wasn't much, but it was home. It was unpainted clapboard inside and out. Newspaper served as wallpaper and pictures from catalogs and calendars from the dime store hung on the walls. There was no indoor plumbing except for the kitchen pump Lavada had bartered for when she could no longer carry water from outside.

The outhouse was located way at the back of the property, down a rocky hill at the edge of the woods. When nature called, it was no easy task for either to relieve themselves. A slop jar under the bed kept them from cold night visits which could worsen their rheumatism.

Delbert and Lavada had a small garden and a few chickens, which met their daily nutritional needs. Mostly, they ate eggs, vegetables, biscuits with gravy, and fish that Delbert caught. Sunday dinner was the main meal each week.

Every Sunday, Lavada grumbled, "Delbert, hurry up. We're gonna be late for the preachin'."

"I'm a-hurryin'," Delbert replied, who didn't know the meaning of the word hurry. Lavada insisted he attend the Holiness Foursquare Church each Sunday, after which she would fix fried chicken, mashed potatoes and gravy, corn or okra, and Delbert's favorite, orange Jell-O with shredded carrots, raisins, and sometimes canned pineapple when money was available. Dessert was rhubarb or gooseberry pie, both made fresh from the garden.

"That was mighty good, Lavada, and there's enough left for supper. I love cold chicken and leftover pie," sighed Delbert, rubbing his ample stomach.

After supper, they would settle down and listen to the radio, next to the wood-burning stove in the front room. Both were huge baseball fans. If the Saint Louis Cardinals, the south's only professional team until almost a decade later, were playing, their ears were glued to the set. Lavada would loudly repeat everything the announcer said for Delbert, who insisted he could have heard if not for the ball park noises and static on the radio. Together, they would hoot and holler when Stan "The Man" Musial hit a double or sometimes "Old Number 6" would hit it out of the ballpark for a home run.

"Are we goin' to the high school game on Saturday?" asked Delbert.

"Have I ever let you miss a game?" groused Lavada. They never got to a professional game, but they never missed the local high school games.

When Lavada became sick, she ignored it and

carried on until she was taken off to the hospital in an ambulance. Delbert was left to fend for himself in the rundown house. Townspeople came by from time to time to drop off a casserole or drive him to visit Lavada in the hospital. "I miss you, Sis. Old Number 6 hit a triple last night and everyone just went crazy. I couldn't understand a word that was said. I miss your cookin', Sister. When are you comin' home?" But Lavada never did come home. After she passed, Delbert had such a hard time caring for himself that he became depressed and lost his famous smile.

His only living relative, a niece, Lavinia's daughter, lived in California. She tried to get him to come live with her, but he would have none of it. "There's a lovely assisted living residence near me." He balked at that idea too. "At Balboa Shores, they would provide a comfortable room for you, and all your meals. And there's a TV, so you could actually see Stan the Man and the rest of the Cardinals play." That sounded pretty good to Delbert. Then his niece reintroduced Coldale Bank's buyout proposal.

After much persuading, Delbert, wearing his best bib overalls and engineer's hat, found himself sitting with his niece in the office of the bank manager. They negotiated the sale of the only home he'd ever known and set up a trust fund from which his niece would pay Balboa Shores every month for his care.

"Uncle Delbert, I'm sure you're going to love it there. And I'll be able to visit more often." Delbert nodded, but his eyes remained wary and he had only a ghost of his famous smile.

* * *

He was now looking forward to Thanksgiving, and enjoying his life at Balboa Shores enough to joke with Patsy. Delbert had found a kindred soul in Sarah. They had developed a friendship that suited them both, quiet and easy – that is, when Catherine wasn't hovering around.

CHAPTER 19

To allow relatives to spend the holidays at their own homes and still celebrate with loved ones at Balboa Shores, Thanksgiving dinner was served the Sunday before the holiday. Cornucopias filled with squash, mums, and fall leaves of every color stood in the center of each table, surrounded by Balboa Shores' best crystal and china.

A buffet was served, and the staff carried plates for residents who needed help. Patsy smiled as she overheard Delbert telling his niece, "You know, where I grew up, it was so cold by Thanksgiving we bought milk by the pound."

Laughter streamed from Miss Millie's table as she told her teenage granddaughters her beliefs on how innocent kissing could lead to something more serious. "I call it my popcorn theory. If you heat popcorn to a certain temperature, it's going to start popping and it won't stop popping until it's all popped out. Nothing you can do will stop it – once it starts popping, you better watch out!"

Casey Howell was there to eat with his father. At the Gerrick's table, a tense feeling hung in the air as Fannie and her daughters visited while Peter sat and ate in silence. Beatrice sat with her son, John, and her daughter, Joan. Patsy arranged for residents without family to sit together at the main table. Sarah and Catherine had the company of Maisie, Alletta, and Olga.

"Happy holidays!" Maisie sang as she approached the table. She passed around the gifts she had brought; apparently no wrapping was necessary. There was a can of tuna for Olga, stamps for Alletta, a half-full can of coffee for Catherine, and a baby doll for Sarah.

Olga sighed. "You didn't tell me we were supposed to bring gifts."

"It's a little early for Christmas, isn't it?" scoffed Catherine.

Sarah reached out to pat Maisie's hand. "A gift is always a nice thought. Thank you so much. I always wanted a baby girl."

Olga clapped her hands in delight. "Fish, my favorite."

Catherine looked at the brown half-full can of coffee like it was a large dog turd. Maisie put her hands together, clearly pleased with herself. "You are all quite welcome." Taking her plate, Maisie started toward the buffet table.

When everyone had gone through the buffet line, Susan Jackson stood and spoke to the group. "I just want to say how wonderful it is to have such a great turnout for our Thanksgiving dinner. We are thankful for each of you who made a special effort to be with our family today. I hope you enjoy the buffet, the music, and most of all each other. Have a wonderful day." The violinist, hired especially for the dinner, started playing chamber music, lending a soft calm to the atmosphere.

As Patsy passed Harry's table, he rose halfway from his chair. "Happy Thanksgiving, darlin'. You're looking lovely today. Have you met my son?"

Casey rolled his eyes. "Yes, Dad, we've met."

"Good," said Harry. "You're my two favorite people, you know."

Patsy and Casey made eye contact, but avoided any pretense of conversation. "Harry, I hope you and your son are enjoying your dinner," Patsy said as she turned to go.

"We'd enjoy it more if you'd sit with us," said Harry.

"I'd love to, Harry, but I have some things still to take care of. Some other time, maybe?"

Harry looked crestfallen. "But how are you two going to get to know each other if you don't spend some time together?"

Casey looked up. "Dad, I think I know Miss Smith as well if not better than you do."

Patsy couldn't believe her ears. "Have a great Thanksgiving, Harry."

CHAPTER 20
SARAH ELIZABETH OWEN
INDIA, 1926

Sarah disliked the bazaar atmosphere. The filthy streets strewn with rubbish and debris made her sick to her stomach. She was disgusted by the lack of hygienic toilet facilities and the number of men urinating beside the stalls. The poor were constantly begging for rupees she did not have. The rampant poverty and sickness overwhelmed her.

She refrained from alerting her family to the not-so-beautiful animals of India. The sound of the hyenas harsh laughter sent chills through her spine. Her family would not be comforted by the knowledge that hyenas sometimes dragged young babies out of family huts and devoured them. Whenever Aja came across the tracks of the blunt-nosed, armor-plated crocodiles called muggers, she would grab Sarah and make a hasty retreat away from the river to higher ground. The muggers' tracks were easy to recognize by the elongated smears in the river mud, with deep grooves on either side made by their vicious claws. Even though the village parents had strongly advised their children to stay away from the rivers edge, the adventurous ones would lie flat, hidden in the grass a good distance away, and wait for the muggers to crawl out of the water.

After a few hours spent walking through the bazaar passing out tracts, Sarah stopped to drink from her canteen and to wipe the mixture of sweat and dirt from her face. The soft sound of a child wailing caught her attention. Her eyes followed him as he ran into the center of the crowd, approaching one man after another, frantically pleading, "Please sir, come help my master. He's bleeding bad. His foot, a turtle bit it. There's a large hole. Please, hurry." No one paid attention to him. Vendors brushed him away from their stalls before he could distract their buyers.

Sarah, who still only spoke little Hindi, asked Aja what the boy was saying. When she heard his tale, she said, "Tell him we'll go with him." Sarah and Aja followed the boy a short ways from the bazaar and over a rise to the river. They came across another young boy crying. He was dressed in fine embroidered silk, a gaping hole in his foot.

Sarah knelt down and used water from her canteen to clean the wound, quietly comforting the boy as she worked. Aja told her his name was Kavi. "Kavi, you're going to be all right," Sarah spoke to the boy, assuring him that he was safe. Aja interpreted as Sarah took off her cotton underskirt and tore a clean piece to bind the boy's foot.

Then, with the few rupees she had for emergencies, she hired a dandy, a modest chair carried on the shoulders of four porters, and took the boy back to the mission compound where she knew she'd find disinfectants and antibiotics. There, she cleaned and rewrapped the wound in bandages, hoping to keep infection from setting in before it had a chance to heal. She sent Aja with the boy's servant to fetch the father and bring him to the mission.

The young servant ran ahead of the procession, announcing the arrival of the boy's father. The older man was elegant in dress and manner as he stepped out of the palanquin carried by four elaborately dressed servants. This was Sarah's introduction to the royalty of India's Princely States.

Kavi's father was a Rajah. His turban, beard, and sword gave him a sinister look; however, his eyes were kind and his voice, soft and gentle. He held her hand, speaking English with a British accent, as he told her how grateful he was for helping his son. He asked Sarah to show him around the mission station. Sarah took the Rajah on a tour of the mission's spartan facility.

"These people need so much more than tracts and the little medicine available at the mission,"

Sarah explained. "I do what I can to help, but I worry that my skills are not enough to deal with such problems. We should have more doctors and qualified nurses to help the locals with their physical needs before they can even think about a foreign God's love and his son Jesus. These Hindu women think that throwing themselves on their husband's funeral pyres is love. How could a country where sutee is not only tolerated but honored ever be converted to a Christian God?"

The day after the Rajah visited the mission, the servant boy arrived with a basket of fruit and an invitation for Sarah to accompany him to the home of the Rajah. Sarah readily agreed. As she entered the gold- and jewel-encrusted palace, her eyes didn't know where to look first. She was met by Rajah Kapur Sinn and Kavi in one of the receiving rooms. The Rajah again thanked her for her kindness to his son, and asked if there was anything she or the mission needed.

Sarah paused, so many possibilities racing through her mind. Then her eyes lit up, she clapped her hands and said, "Books, medical books, supplies and training." Her excitement caught everyone by surprise. Sarah hadn't realized until that moment that nursing, not tracts, was her destiny.

The Rajah, impressed with her fervent passion, stood and declared, "You are truly a remarkable young woman. Not only will I see that you get all the medical books you need, I will send you to Delhi to the British Hospital for whatever training they provide." Rising and standing to his full stature, he proclaimed, "It will be done!"

* * *

Sarah completed a six-month course of nursing in Delhi and returned with a large stockpile of medical reference books. She took over many of the medical duties at the mission, with more than adequate supplies due to the generosity of the Rajah. Sarah used her newfound skills to venture outside the compound, visiting remote villages and assisting those who could not travel to the mission on their own.

Kavi's young servant was named Chatur. He and Aja accompanied Sarah on her treks into the countryside. Chatur was helpful, clever, and so enthusiastic. He told Sarah of his desire to one day become a doctor, and of his sorrow that it was not a possibility because of his caste. Sarah assured him that nothing was impossible with God. *I will talk with the Rajah,* she decided.

The Rajah sent Chatur to England along with his own son, the former to obtain a medical degree, the latter to receive a gentleman's education.

In later years as the Rajah's health deteriorated, Sarah made many trips to the palace. Ever faithful Chatur was there to ease the end of the Rajah's life. Sarah was also there to comfort him. Kavi followed in his father's footsteps and continued to support Sarah's work at the mission hospital, making it possible for her and Chatur to travel to leper colonies. They did what they could to alleviate the suffering and ostracizing of those poor untouchable souls. Sarah no longer flinched at the poverty nor the unsanitary conditions. She had come to love India and it's people. For her faithful, loving care she earned the name *Mata Sarah* or *gentle mother*.

At times, Sarah became despondent that the opportunity for love and family in this foreign country never came her way. Many times, while holding and caring for an infant, she would feel the overwhelming desire to put the child to her own breast. In time she came to reconcile her sometimes lonely life with the greater good that she knew she had accomplished. The aging Sarah found contentment in giving her life to India and its people.

Sarah was still serving in India on her eightieth

birthday. Though quite agile, she was becoming forgetful, often not remembering the names of frequent visitors, or forgetting the appropriate protocol for familiar procedures. The trips to other villages were becoming more taxing and she often forgot to take along a needed medicine or piece of equipment.

She had come to India during the British Rule and stayed through Gandhi's struggle for independence. She had covered her ears and trembled as she carried on her work in the midst of gunfire and riots, provoked by the intolerance of the Muslim and Hindi religions, until India became divided and gave Muslims their own country. Through it all, she had been steadfast. She had earned her retirement, but didn't understand why her health dictated a return to the United States. She would have been happy to live out her life in her beloved India. The mission home in Wisconsin was offered up to her, but Chatur, while conferring with colleagues in the United States the year before, had visited an assisted living facility in a warmer climate not so different from India. When told about Balboa Shores, Kavi insisted it was where Sarah should go. Kavi would finance her stay for as long as she needed.

CHAPTER 21
DECEMBER

Christmas was fast approaching, and every inch of Balboa Shores was decorated. A twenty-foot tree graced the foyer; a garland with red berries and bows wound around the rail of the staircase. The fireplace crackled and Christmas music filled the air. The aroma from the platter of fresh-baked cookies mingled with the scent of pine.

Patsy was in the Activities Room helping a group make paper chains of red, green, and silver.

"I haven't made these since I was a little girl," said Miss Millie. "We always had homemade decorations on our tree."

Patsy smiled at her. "I thought about doing popcorn and cranberry strings, but I tried it at home and I stuck myself with the needle so often that I didn't want you to do the same. So paper chains will be our contribution to an old-fashioned Christmas."

The decoration table was set up so residents could come and go as they pleased. At first Patsy had planned to do a red-silver-green pattern, but that quickly went awry and the results looked just as festive. When a pile of chains accumulated, she would piece them together and hang them down the hallways.

Patsy was also collecting donations for the Children's Hospital. She asked if the residents would like to give cash or maybe buy something at the bingo auction, a new stuffed animal or doll perhaps, to contribute.

Miss Millie stopped her in the hall. "I bought the cutest little panda bear at the bingo auction some time ago, and had it up on my china hutch. I was going to donate it, but now I can't find it. I also had some note cards I thought would do, but they're gone too. I must be getting old, Patsy. I don't remember using all those note cards. Well, never mind that now. I'll be happy to give you twenty dollars for the Children's Hospital."

Overhearing the conversation, Olga approached. "Miss Millie, I think Beatrice has your panda."

"Why would she have my panda?"

"Who knows why Beatrice does anything? She had a panda in her arms when she passed by my room the other day. I said 'How cute Beatrice, where did you get that?' And you know what she said?" Olga raised her eyebrows. "She said she *found* it. I asked where, and she told me it was none of my business." Olga shook her head.

Miss Millie looked confused. "She's always carrying new things in her walker. Where does she find it all?"

"No, she *takes* things!" Olga said in her loud piercing voice. "Have you seen all the stuff she has in her room? I saw her pick up something at the bingo table that she didn't buy. I told her it wasn't hers, but she just hugged it to her bosom and said, 'No, it *is* mine.'"

Patsy tried to calm her. "I'll take care of it, Olga. Please, you shouldn't be accusing anyone."

Patsy made a point of stopping by Beatrice's room before she left for the day. It was a mess, and true enough, a stuffed panda lay face-down on her bed, along with a menagerie of other animals. Beatrice looked sheepishly at Patsy. "I love my animals."

"I know you do, Beatrice. But where did you get all these since we cleaned up your room last fall?"

"I don't know. They kinda found me. I guess they needed a home."

"You know what I think? I think the Children's Hospital would be a good home to some of your stuffed animals. Keep the ones you've had for a long time, but the ones that are still in boxes and have tags on them would make the children so happy. It would be such a kind thing to do at Christmas." Patsy moved the panda and sat down on Beatrice's bed.

Beatrice looked crushed. "I can't give them

away. I won't have any for myself."

"What if I just take this panda for now?" coaxed Patsy. "Look, it still has the price tag on it. We can talk about the rest later. Beatrice, the children will give it tons of love and you'll always know where it is." Beatrice tearfully agreed to let the panda go.

* * *

The holiday party fell on the Sunday before Christmas. Everyone who was well enough got dressed in their holiday best and came to have a Polaroid picture taken with Santa. Residents sat on his lap in front of the huge tree and walked away with a framed picture. Alletta put her arms around Santa and, just as the camera snapped, kissed him on the forehead. When it was Beatrice's turn, she blushed so much that her cheeks almost matched Santa's suit. Fannie looked rested and happier than she had in weeks. Alletta came back for more, declaring, "I haven't had my picture with Santa yet." Patsy was quite sure she had, but happily agreed to take it again.

Alletta climbed up on his lap. "Hi, Santa. I've been really a really good girl this year. Do I get a kiss?" Santa put his arms around her and obligingly gave her a kiss on the cheek.

143

As Santa got ready to depart, the group gathered for a hand bell concert in the Great Room when Alletta showed up again.

"I want a picture with Santa Claus," she declared.

"Alletta, you've already had two," said Patsy.

"No, I haven't. I want to get my picture with him like everyone else."

Third time's a charm, thought Patsy, as she ushered Alletta to Santa's lap for a final time, then pried her off him and sat her down for the concert.

Sarah had received word from Kavi that he would visit this Christmas. He had not been to the US in several years, and he was eager to spend Christmas with Sarah once again. He sat with Sarah next to Delbert and Jack. Sarah held her Christmas present from Delbert, a single poinsettia. Delbert was smiling and enjoying the beat of the music. At every ring of a bell, Jack would let out a triumphant bark. After a few songs, residents began shushing Jack and throwing Delbert nasty looks. Patsy took Jack by the leash and told Delbert that the dog would be in the office and he could retrieve him after the concert.

Dinner was a festive occasion. Candles and champagne were on every table. The delicious smell of roast beef au jus warmed the dining room.

Yorkshire pudding, brussels sprouts, and a chocolate Yule log cake completed the meal.

Kavi sat at the main table with Sarah, and they were joined by Catherine, Delbert and his neice, Alletta, Harry, and Casey. Beatrice and Maisie sat together. Miss Millie sat with her daughter and granddaughters along with Fannie and Peter Gerrick. Patsy looked across the sea of faces. Everyone had someone with whom to share the holiday meal. Even if there was not peace on earth, there was peace and love in this room tonight.

CHAPTER 22
JANUARY

Patsy was getting ready for the monthly reception for new Balboa Shores residents. She carried the large punch bowl from the kitchen to the Great Room. After making sure she had enough cups and napkins on the table, she lit the gas fireplace and turned it to low, then set out the trays of hors d'oeuvres. While she was arranging the chairs around the piano, her attention was drawn to a commotion in the hallway. Peter Gerrick was arguing with his wife, Fannie.

"I don't want to go. Do you hear me? I don't want to sit around with a bunch of people I don't know and don't care to know. You may be my wife, but you can't tell me what to do."

"Peter, please don't yell," Fannie pleaded from her wheelchair. "You're embarrassing me."

"I'm not yelling, I'm just raising my voice."

"Well, then, lower your voice please. Can't you do something for me just this once?"

"You forget about all I do for you around here. That skilled nursing spoiled you. If it weren't for me, you'd be in a nursing home."

"I know dear, you help me an awful lot. But occasionally, couldn't you do something I want without being such a grouch?"

With that, Peter turned on his heels and headed for the door. "I'm going for a drive. Maybe I'll see you at dinner. You can have your paid caretaker take you back up to the room."

"Peter, please don't drive. You know you're not supposed to anymore."

"Let's not start on that, Fannie. I drive better than any of those irresponsible teenagers on the roads today, that's for sure."

"It's not a matter of being responsible. I know you are, but your strength and reaction time aren't what they used to be."

"Hogwash! I can still drive to Vegas any day of the week. Today just might be that day." Peter stomped out, leaving Fannie sitting silently in her wheelchair in the hallway.

Grabbing the handles of the wheelchair, Patsy bent down close to Fannie. "If you're ready, Fannie, I'll take you to the Great Room. Try not to worry about Peter. Give him some time to cool down. Men are funny that way. He'll probably bring you flowers when he comes back."

"Oh my, Patsy, you really are a romantic. No, not my Peter. You don't know him the way I do. He's too cheap to buy flowers, and if he did I really *would* be worried." Residents were starting to arrive, so Patsy parked Fannie's chair close to the front.

Patsy spotted Casey Howell walking in with his father, and she felt her stomach start to churn. *Wait, what is this? Butterflies?* He was undeniably good-looking, that was for sure. *Heaven forbid,* she thought. Whatever the cause, she was determined not to make eye contact or respond to him in any way. She directed her energy toward the new residents.

Susan Jackson took the microphone and welcomed everyone. "We have two new residents today. I'd like to introduce Dr. and Mrs. Moore." Glancing at a three by five index card, she continued. "The Moores come to us from their home of 32 years in Charleston, South Carolina. Dr. Moore spent time in the Navy as a medical corpsman, and then went on to get his medical degree at the University of Virginia. He practiced family medicine and spent some time in the back country of the Appalachian Mountains. He met and married his wife while in medical school. According to Dr. Moore, she was the cutest of all the student nurses. She maintained the office and was his nurse until their firstborn came along. They have three children, all girls. One lives here in our community and is with us today." Looking at their daughter, Susan added, "We are very pleased to have you here and hope you feel welcome to drop in at any time and visit."

Harry Howell, a long-time friend of the Moore family, stood up to welcome them with one of their favorite songs. Harry patted Dr. Moore on the back and shook hands with Mrs. Moore, then began singing "Carolina Moon" in a beautiful tenor voice. When he finished he received tremendous applause, after which Susan encouraged everyone to have some refreshments, mingle, and take time to get to know the new residents.

Patsy approached Harry after the song. "Harry, you really have a beautiful voice."

"Thank you, darlin'," Harry said in response.

Patsy smiled. "I didn't know you were friends with the Moores. What a nice way to welcome them to Balboa Shores."

Casey responded, "Our company built some medical offices for Dr. Moore's son-in-law. My dad and he became good friends."

Harry broke in. "I guess this is as good a time as any to tell you about Patsy. Casey, this is Miss Patsy Smith, the young lady I was telling you about. This is the one I'm hoping to make the next Mrs. Howell."

"WHAT?!" exclaimed Casey and Patsy in unison. It was Casey who spoke first. "*This* is the woman you're in love with?"

Patsy interrupted. "Wait just a minute, Mr. Howell. Both Mr. Howells. I have no intention of marrying anyone, particularly not anyone standing here. Harry, what made you think such a thing?"

Harry gave a sheepish grin. "Well, I hadn't quite got around to asking you yet, but you must know how I feel about you, Patsy. I kind of figured you felt the same way, since you're always so sweet to me and we get along so well."

"We get along so well because you are a charming man, Harry Howell. And I am extremely fond of you, but not in a romantic way. Harry, why did you tell your son you were going to marry me?"

"Because I love you and I want to marry you."

Patsy rubbed her temples. "Some time ago, your son came to Ms. Jackson to warn her about an individual you were becoming involved with. We naturally assumed it was one of the other residents. Was it me you were talking about?"

"Who else would it be?" smiled Harry.

"Oh Harry! I can't believe you thought I'd marry you."

"Don't say that, Patsy. You must know how I feel about you."

"No, I didn't have any idea you felt more than friendship for me. I like you a lot, but I don't love you, and I have no intention of getting involved with you. This is where I work and I just couldn't do that. It wouldn't be right."

"I don't care what it looks like or what my son thinks."

"Well, I care what your son thinks and I care about my job and all the people in this home. Let's go to Ms. Jackson's office and talk about this." Patsy took Harry by the arm and Casey followed. She knocked softly at the director's door.

"Come in."

"Ms. Jackson, we need to clear up a terrible misunderstanding. Harry just told his son that I'm the one he's been talking about marrying." Turning to Casey, she continued. "Mr. Howell, believe me, I had no idea when you told us about your father's interest in one of the ladies here that it was me. He is a wonderful man, but he misinterpreted my attention and its meaning. I would never lead someone on, especially a resident in my care." Turning back to Harry, Patsy's voice softened. "I'm sorry, Harry. I don't mean to hurt your feelings, but I must tell you that our relationship is purely platonic."

Harry looked crushed. "I don't know why my son is so upset by all this. I thought he'd be pleased. I thought he'd love you as much as I love you," explained Harry.

Patsy turned to the younger Howell. "Casey, do you understand that this whole marriage scenario was a product of your father's dementia? It wasn't based in reality. My concern for your father as a dear, dear person got mixed up in his head."

At first Casey said nothing, looking down in shame. When at last he looked up, he looked Patsy in the eye. "Miss Smith, I apologize for the misunderstanding. I'm afraid I sometimes overreact and my temper gets the best of me. I can be ... well, frankly, I can be a colossal ass sometimes. I know Dad lives in a fantasy world. I don't know why I thought you were the one trying to entrap him. I really do owe you an apology."

Patsy, touched at the turnaround in Casey, sighed in relief. "Of course I accept your apology. And Harry, I apologize to you if I did anything to give you the wrong impression of our friendship." Harry just sat there, looking crestfallen. Casey got up, shook hands with Susan and Patsy, and gently led his father out of the office.

* * *

Patsy was surprised that evening to receive a call from Casey. "Hello, Patsy. May I call you Patsy? I wanted to apologize again for my poor behavior. I was hoping you'd let me make it up to you by taking you to dinner."

"That's very generous of you, Mr. Howell ..."

"Please, call me Casey."

"That's very generous of you, Casey, but completely unnecessary. There's no need to make anything up to me."

"Even so, I would like to have dinner with you."

"That's very kind of you, but it's a bit hard to believe. You haven't even acknowledged me for the last month when you've come to see your father. Listen, I accept your apology, and I'm glad to know you're not still upset. But you don't owe me anything."

"I told you I'm hard-headed, and I do feel I owe you at least dinner."

"Actually, if memory serves, I think your exact words were 'colossal ass.'" Patsy heard a slight chuckle from the other end of the phone.

"You're right, colossal ass it is." He paused. "I really want to take you to dinner. Would Saturday night work?"

Patsy sighed. He was really trying, and she did find him attractive, so why not? "As long as you don't take me to Denim and Diamonds, it's a date."

CHAPTER 23

"It's Monday, so it's bingo night," Peter Gerrick told Fannie, and without another word, left her sitting in her wheelchair at the dinner table, assuming someone would wheel her back to the apartment.

In her one-bedroom apartment, Fannie sat on the couch with her feet propped up on two pillows to alleviate the dull ache in her hip. She pulled the soft pink angora afghan around her to ease the chill. The blanket was the same one Olga knitted for her the last time Fannie had been in the skilled nursing unit with a broken arm. Dusk was beginning to fall, casting shadows on the side tables laden with knick knacks. The radio played softly.

After dinner, Patsy knocked on the door and opened it a crack. "Hi, Fannie. May I come in for a moment?"

Fannie's eyes were closed and, to most, she probably looked like she was at peace with the world. But Patsy sensed that more was going on, and looking at Fannie, she saw a weary and despondent wife, sitting alone amidst a few remaining mementos from a happier time.

Without opening her eyes, Fannie whispered, "Sure, Patsy, come on in. I'm alone as you can see."

Patsy chose a footstool close to the sofa and sat down. "I wanted to see how you're doing and if Peter is taking good care of you."

"Peter? He's down playing bingo. When he's around, he fetches me water and sometimes helps me to the bathroom. Other times he has me call a caregiver. We hardly ever talk anymore."

"What about physical things? I mean, has he ever raised his hand to you or hurt you? Has he ever done anything that caused you injury?"

"Oh, Patsy, what makes you think that? Anyway, it's all water under the bridge. Peter doesn't mean to lose his temper. Sometimes he shoves me or pushes me a little. When I was younger, I could handle it better than I do now. My balance isn't what it used to be, so sometimes I trip or fall down."

"We've all witnessed Peter's temper, Fannie, but under no circumstances should he be pushing or shoving you. It was only six months ago that you broke your arm, and your broken hip happening so soon just seems like too much of a coincidence. It makes me uneasy. I want you to know that I have to report my concerns to Ms. Jackson."

Leaning forward, Fannie pleaded, "Patsy, please. I don't want to leave here and if Peter is made to leave, I'll have to go with him."

"That's not necessarily true." Patting Fannie's

leg, Patsy asked, "Do any of your children know how you broke these bones?"

"No, and I don't want them to know. I'm happy here and I don't want my children worrying that I'm not being taken care of. And Peter's kids don't give a hoot."

"Fannie, if Peter is hurting you, we have to do something about it."

Fannie closed her eyes again and told Patsy she was tired. Patsy put her arms around Fannie, smoothed her hair, told her to sleep tight, and quietly left the apartment.

Downstairs in the Activities Room, the bingo cards had been set up for the evening game. Two cards per person was the limit, and winners received the coveted Bingo Bucks. One of the staff members was rolling the cage, testing it to make sure only one ball came down the chute at a time. By 6:15 the room was full.

The caller shouted enthusiastically, "Everyone ready to play?" Olga asked if she could play a couple cards for Beatrice, who wasn't feeling well at dinner but hated to miss the opportunity to win Bingo Bucks. The caller asked if anyone objected. Peter rose and loudly exclaimed, "If Olga gets to play for Beatrice, then I get to play for Fannie."

"But Fannie never comes to bingo and Beatrice

plays all the time," protested Olga, her Swedish accent raging.

"Fair is fair, Olga," Peter insisted. "If one of us can do it then we all should be able to. Otherwise someone will be getting extra Bingo Bucks."

Olga stood up to confront Peter across the bingo table, her owlish eyes glaring through her thick glasses. "When have you ever worried about fair, you silly old man? They're not my Bingo Bucks. They're for Beatrice."

Resting his hands on the table and leaning toward Olga, nose to nose, Peter retorted, "That's what you say, but what's to stop you from keeping them all for yourself?"

Miss Millie stood up. "Calm down, both of you," she ordered. "I want to play bingo."

The bingo caller tried to intervene. "Olga, as long as we have a two-card limit, I'll have to hold you to that. If you want to change the rules you can take it to the residents' council."

Still in a snit, Olga and Peter returned to their seats as the first number was called. "B9. Be mine, B nine."

CHAPTER 24
FANNIE GERRICK
CALIFORNIA, 1920

Tuesday found Fannie sitting in her wheelchair in the healing garden, her eyes closed, listening to the sound of water trickling over rocks into the small pond below. It brought her back to her childhood in the foothills of the Sierra Mountains. The calming sound of mountain streams had always brought peace to her soul and her mind. She'd had a good life, she supposed, not perfect but good. The three men in her life had been so different from each other, yet she loved each of them in spite of their flaws.

Her father, Ed, worked for the railroad and always provided for his family. The pay was low and her parents had to be careful with their money when she was young.

"Daddy, can we please go get ice cream after dinner?" Her father loved ice cream, and relished the act of taking his daughter to the drug store that sold cones for five cents a scoop.

"Did you do your chores today?" If she didn't dust the living room end tables enough, he would write the date in the dust and take her to see it several days later.

"Yes, Daddy."

"Good girl. Yes, we'll go for ice cream after dinner." He smiled as he patted her head.

Ice cream and parades, those were her favorite childhood memories. Vacations were always the same, visiting relatives in the Midwest. Her father got a free ticket once a year on the second-class passenger train. As a teenager, Fannie loved the three-day train trip because of all the service men she met in the club car, where the soldiers played cards and drank beer. She purposely chose ginger ale, thinking it looked more like liquor and would make her seem more sophisticated.

Once at their destination, their food and lodging would be provided by her aunts and uncles. Entertainment was boat rides on the lake and picnics. Popcorn, board games, homemade ice cream, and chasing fireflies filled the evenings. The special treat was going to her uncle's toy store after hours and getting to pick one thing, anything she wanted.

The few arguments her parents had were over money and flirtations. "What do you think I did with the money? Spend it on some floozy?" was her father's reply to his wife's questioning. Her mother was gregarious, talkative, passionate and flirtatious. She liked being the center of attention. Her father had been quiet, introspective, and immaculate in his dress and grooming. He was discreet, but flirted with the women in their square dance group and sometimes carried it beyond what met the eye. Each was jealous of the other, a love-hate relationship, but both were dedicated to their daughter. Ed's little girl had him wrapped around her little finger. "This hurts me more than it does you," he would say after spankings that her mother instigated.

Fannie's mother was the one with the business sense. She saved the family a substantial amount of money by subcontracting work on their new house to down-and-outers who hung around the railroad station. She was able to build a seven thousand dollar house for three thousand and, after living in it for two years, sold it for eight thousand. With this tidy sum, she bought several small fixer-upper duplexes near the railroad tracks. Her knack for good real estate buys served as a springboard into more expensive rental properties.

Neither parent attended college, and both were adamant that their child would do so. College was expected of Fannie, and the extra income from the rentals made it possible.

Away at college, Fannie met Frank, the son of a contractor. They hit it off immediately. Frank was studying to be an architect. Marriage followed after college and Fannie got her first real vacation on their honeymoon to Hawaii. They settled down on the west coast and had three precious little girls. Fannie and Frank lived well. Frank had become a success and Fannie gave her full attention to raising her children. They lived in a good neighborhood and had a new car every other year. Each girl got a college degree.

Together, Fannie and Frank kept busy visiting their grandchildren. "We're going to take the motor home to Montana to see our newest grandchild," she told Alice, her only single daughter. It was after returning from one of these trips that Frank felt unusually tired and had bruises covering his arms. The diagnosis was leukemia. He was dead in sixteen months. Fannie was widowed at sixty-four.

Alice came to visit when she could. She was attending law school, whose claim to fame was that it had produced one of the Supreme Court justices. Alice encouraged her mother to get out, attend church, gardening and other club meetings.

It was at an AARP gathering in the park that Fannie met Peter. He was immediately drawn to her, telling her she was the only woman who seemed to be having a good time and that she sparkled more than her two carat diamond ring.

He was handsome and in great physical condition. She was flattered by his attention. He told her he had owned a car dealership, but was now retired. Not until later did she learn he had to sell it due to risky lending and bad investments in the stock market.

"Say, do you play bridge?" asked Peter.

"No, I never had the desire to learn."

"Well, it's my favorite game. You're going to have to learn to play. I think there's a class through AARP."

Fannie enjoyed learning bridge. She would tell Alice, "I just wish they didn't have to be so serious all the time. Peter gets very upset when I talk during games. He says I talk more than I play."

One evening over dinner, Fannie told Peter, "My three daughters and their children will be coming to visit during spring break. I'd like you to meet them and I'd like them to get to know you. You're a very mysterious man to them."

"What's to know? We hit it off and are having a good time together. What have you told them about me?" Peter asked. "Did you tell them about your competition?"

Fannie stopped in mid-bite of her buttered roll. "Competition? I didn't know we were in a contest." Peter told Fannie about another woman, a rich woman, who was trying to get him to marry her.

"She's all furs and opera and stuff like that. Don't worry, she's too old for me. And you're much more fun." Fannie hadn't known he was seeing another woman, and she wasn't sure whether to take his words as a compliment or not.

Fannie, Peter, her kids and grandkids all went out for pizza during Easter week. Peter asked what kind of pizza they liked. The three older grandchildren chimed in. "Cheese and pepperoni." "No, just cheese." "I want sausage." Fannie's eldest daughter, Judy, stepped in and said one combination and one plain cheese would work. Peter ordered a pitcher of soda for the kids. He wanted to know if anyone wanted beer.

Lucy said, "Why don't we get a couple of pitchers for the five adults?"

Peter recoiled. "Don't you think that's a little much? Maybe we should each get a glass. It's less expensive than two pitchers, which we probably wouldn't finish anyway."

Alice, the middle daughter, sighed and said, "What if I buy the beer and you buy the pizza?"

"Sounds fair," said Peter, adjusting his glasses. "If you buy the drinks then you can get two pitchers of beer and two of soda for the kids if you want."

Alice rolled her eyes, which elicited raised

eyebrows from the other two sisters.

At home later that night, Fannie sat with Lucy. "Well, what do you think of my new friend?"

"Is that all he is, Mom, a friend?"

"No, it's more than that. He wants to move in with me and rent out his place. I told him I wouldn't live with him. If he wants to live together we would have to be married."

"Are you considering marriage?"

"I've been lonely without your dad. You know I would have nursed him the rest of my life if he had lived. But he's gone, and being with Peter is exciting. It's like being young again."

"Have you met his family?"

"No, he tells me they're not as close as our family. They do their thing and he does his."

Lucy sighed. "Two things, Mom. I think you should meet his children before making any decisions. And ... I'm not sure he'd be generous enough for you."

"He's thrifty, like me. We both grew up during the Depression. He's careful with his money. We both have our own investments and we would probably keep them separate. I don't know Peter's situation, but I do trust him."

Lucy hugged her mom. "I want you to be happy, Mom. We had such a wonderful father and you were a team. Think about it, that's all I ask."

CHAPER 25

Following Patsy's talk with Fannie, she sat in Susan Jackson's office with the door closed and related her suspicions that Peter was the cause of Fannie's last two broken bones.

"Why don't you stay here while I call Fannie's daughter? I'll put her on speaker phone and we can ask a little more about their history." Patsy sat back and tried to relax. She tried to think about her upcoming date with Casey Howell until Fannie's daughter, Alice, answered the phone.

"Hello Alice, this is Susan Jackson, director of Balboa Shores."

"Oh, Miss Jackson. Is there something wrong?"

"We're not sure, Alice. I need to talk to you about your father, Peter."

Alice's reply was terse. "He's not my father, Miss Jackson. He's my mother's second husband. What's up with him now?"

Susan wound the telephone cord tightly around her finger. "I need to ask some questions that may sound a little invasive, but my concern is for your mother. Can you tell me if Peter has ever abused her, either physically or verbally?"

Alice launched into a laundry list of complaints. "Peter has abused Mom their entire marriage, but it's gotten worse as he's getting older. We call him The Grumpy Old Bastard, and that's being kind. He's not very well liked in our family." She paused before continuing. "He gets very angry if she uses anything of his, even something small like a pen. He complains constantly about not having enough money to help pay the rent at your place, but he won't share any information about his finances. He knows all about Mom's finances because he opens all her mail."

"What else can you tell us?"

"He has hardly any relationship with his own two children. They come to see him once a year on his birthday. He walked out on Mom several times before they came to Balboa Shores. He'd be gone for two or three days and then he always came back and acted as if nothing had happened. I think the only reason he came back was because he got tired of paying for his own meals and housing. Really, don't get me started."

Dismayed but not surprised, Susan asked, "What about physical abuse, Alice? Have you witnessed any or has your mom shared anything like that with you?"

"He's shoved her and made her fall. I've witnessed that, but she always makes excuses for him. Like 'oh, it was my fault, I can't pick up my feet anymore,' or 'he's upset, he'll calm down and everything will be fine.' And I've noticed a few bruises here and there."

"Well, she may have only bruised before, but not she's much more frail and her balance isn't so good. I'm concerned that he might have pushed her and caused the two broken bones she's had in the last six months. It seems to be getting worse. First an arm and now a hip. Fannie talked with one of our caregivers, and she got very anxious when the topic of potential abuse came up. She was afraid she would have to move, and said Peter didn't mean to push her, she just lost her balance and fell."

"I've heard that before, but never really connected it to her fractures until now. What should we do?" asked Alice.

"I'm afraid I must inform Adult Protective Services and someone will come out and conduct an investigation."

"I think that's a good idea. Mom won't be able to blame the family for what may or may not happen. I know she'll be upset, but it's the right thing to do."

"It's not only the right thing to do, Alice, it's the law. I'm required to report any suspicion of abuse," Susan said. "It protects Balboa Shores. Some family members might accuse us of causing these accidents and get us into legal trouble."

"I know it wasn't your fault. We all think you give Mom the best care."

Susan untangled her fingers from the telephone cord. "Thank you, Alice. I wish all families could be like yours. I'm glad we had this talk and I understand that you want the best for your mother. We do too, and that might mean confronting Peter and taking steps to prevent any further problems. Thank you for your help, I'll keep you posted." Still holding the receiver, Susan pushed the disconnect button and turned to Patsy.

"Why don't we call Dr. Neil and run this by him?" Patsy concurred, and a second call was placed.

After the usual pleasantries, Susan explained her concerns to the doctor. Dr. Neil assured her, "We always ask about spousal abuse when taking a medical history. I can't confirm or deny what I know about this patient, but I would advise you to follow not just the letter of the law but also your instincts."

Thank you, Dr. Neil. I appreciate your advice and support."

In her final phone call of the afternoon, Susan spoke to APS and explained that the information came from Fannie's daughter and Fannie, through her caregiver. The department asked that all parties involved write up the information so that it could be included in their report.

CHAPTER 26

At seven-thirty Saturday evening, Patsy opened the door to Casey Howell. He was dressed in khaki pants and a blue dress shirt, and she was delighted by the beautiful bouquet of flowers he was holding.

"Wow, dinner *and* flowers! You certainly do know how to apologize." Taking the flowers, she thanked him. "Let me put these in some water before we go." Patsy placed the vase on her coffee table as the sweet floral smell drifted up towards her. "Where are we going for dinner?" she asked.

"I know a charming little Italian restaurant that I think you're going to like."

From the outside, the restaurant wasn't much to look at, housed in an old factory building, but inside the brick oven and fireplace made for a cozy ambiance, as did the low lights and candled Chianti bottles on the tables.

After they were seated, Casey said, "You look lovely tonight."

Patsy blushed. She had gone to the trouble of buying a new outfit for this evening and hoped it wasn't obvious she was trying to impress him. "It's a wonder what candlelight will do," she said.

"No need to be so modest. I admit I had doubts about you, but that's because I'm an idiot. You're not a phony and you're certainly not a gold digger. I'm a bit ashamed that I even suggested it. Now that I've gotten that off my chest, would you like a glass of wine?"

"I'm glad you don't feel that way anymore. It's hard for me to grasp that anyone might consider me their enemy. And yes, I would like that glass of wine. Some Merlot sounds wonderful."

When the wine arrived, Casey poured for both of them. "Here's to an evening of burying the hatchet and starting over," he said, raising his glass.

"Hear, hear." Patsy clinked her glass to his.

After ordering, Casey asked softly, "How did a Midwest girl like you end up working in a home for seniors on the west coast?"

Patsy took her time to respond. "My husband was stationed out here in the Marines. I started working at Balboa Shores when he was deployed to Iraq."

"See, I've learned something about you already. I didn't know you'd been married. So you're divorced."

"Widowed. Bud was killed when snipers attacked his convoy. All six in the tank died."

Casey's voice was barely audible. He looked into her eyes and, seeing her sadness, said, "I'm so sorry, Patsy. I had no idea."

"We got married right out of high school. We were very happy for seven years. When it first happened, I didn't think I would make it. But he's been gone three years now. And I have the residents at Balboa Shores to take care of and they help fill the void. I also started going back to school to get my degree. Thought I might want to be a director of a care home, but I can't see leaving our residents." Patsy smiled. "I've become so attached to them; it's probably not healthy."

"The only unhealthy thing about it is you might meet up with more gentlemen who take a fancy to you like my dad. You genuinely care for those folks and they know it. You're the one bright spot in their lives," Casey said.

"Tell me about you, Casey. Have you ever been married?"

"No. No one woman could stand me for any length of time. The one that's brave enough to try hasn't come along yet. In high school I played baseball and took college prep classes. I didn't want to go to college, I wanted to be a big league baseball player. My father expected me to take over and expand his construction business. I got a baseball scholarship to the University of San Diego so I played ball and barely skimmed by with mediocre grades. After graduation, the big leagues showed little interest in me. So, since I had a business degree, I started working for my dad. In reality, the on-the-job training I got during vacations and summers was more helpful than college, but I did learn some things that I implemented into the business plan and they seem to be working out. Now, with Mom gone and Dad unable to run the business, it's up to me to see that Howell and Son carries on."

By the time the *saltimbocca* arrived, Patsy felt she was starting a new and comfortable relationship with Casey Howell.

She wasn't sure she was ready for a dating relationship. Then again, maybe she was making too big a deal out of this. After all, one dinner date wasn't the same as a marriage proposal. When she now thought about Casey and how he'd changed, it made her smile. Then she thought of Bud, and worried that she might be losing the memory of him; it filled her with sorrow.

CHAPTER 27

Susan Jackson received a call that a representative from the State Department of Elder Abuse wanted to meet with Peter Gerrick. She found him playing bridge and asked to speak with him privately. Peter's eyes widened as he resolutely told her no, he would not meet with them. He looked down and shook his head violently. There was no reason and he had no desire to talk to them.

"Mr. Gerrick, they will be here in the morning. I told them you would meet in the library for privacy. I don't think you have a choice, Mr. Gerrick. Don't get upset until you hear what they have to say."

At dinner that evening, Peter and Fannie sat at a table for two in the corner. He was quiet, but that was not unusual. Fannie pushed some carrots around her plate, took a small bite of catfish, and kept her head down through most of the meal.

As Peter licked the last dollop of lemon meringue pie from his fork, Alletta came up behind him and kissed him lightly on the top of his balding head. "It's so rewarding to see a man enjoying his food. Good to see you too, Fannie." As she left the dining room, she looked over her shoulder and gave Peter a little wave and a smile.

Alletta was in her late seventies but looked much

younger. She was petite, very attractive for her age, and affectionate with most of the men at Balboa Shores. It didn't matter if they were married, ambulatory, or just breathing, she would sashay up to them and give each one a kiss, usually on the cheek or the forehead. She had to be watched closely by the staff.

Fannie spoke quietly. "I see you've gotten closer to our friend, Peter."

"Who, Alletta? She is a flirt, now, isn't she?" said Peter, blushing. "Are you jealous? All the women here are jealous of Alletta. She's just a friendly gal. It doesn't mean anything. Leave it alone."

Fannie, not wanting to upset Peter even more, let the subject drop.

The investigator came the following morning and after talking with Ms. Jackson, Patsy, and Fannie, asked to speak with Peter. They met in the library where the doors could be closed for privacy.

When the investigator left, Peter burst into Ms. Jackson's office. The look on his face was livid. "How *dare* you turn me in for abuse! What proof do you have? This is a set-up and I won't stand for it." Peter continued, enraged, "They said they already talked with Fannie and are going to contact her doctor. I won't have that. Keep out of my business if you know what's good for you."

"Mr. Gerrick, as I explained to Fannie earlier, I'm obligated under the law to report any suspicion of abuse. If the investigators find no evidence of mistreatment, nothing will come of it." Peter stormed out, still fuming.

Fannie had lived through many of Peter's temper tantrums, but this one was different. When Peter entered the apartment, it was clear that this outburst was causing him physical distress. His breathing became short and labored, and the veins on his neck and forehead bulged like worms crawling under his flushed skin.

"I've had enough of this, Fannie. I won't stay around and let you frame me. Believe me, this is something I should have done years ago." He grabbed his keys and started for the door.

"Peter, wait! I didn't call. The people in the office must have made the report."

"Well, I don't believe you. It's a vendetta, either by you or one of your spoiled rotten kids. It doesn't matter. I'm done taking care of your pathetic self and getting no appreciation. I'm out of here." The door slammed so hard it shook the apartment.

Peter slid into his new red Coronado and started the engine. His tires screeched as he sped out of the driveway and up the coast road, muttering to himself. "That witch. I've been her chauffeur and gopher for twenty years, and this is the thanks I get? She promised to take care of me for the rest of my life. Some care. Some life. *Peter, get me this. Peter, get me that.* Like I'm her goddamned servant or something. That's what I am, her servant! She should be paying me all the money she's shelling out to her so-called caregivers. I do more for her than any of them ever do."

Pounding his fists on the steering wheel, Peter felt a sudden sharp pain in the front of his head. Closing his eyes as he tried to apply the breaks, he let out a sharp scream as he lost control of the wheel. *Some lousy life* was the last thought running through his head as his vision went black and his car careened off the side of the road.

CHAPTER 28

When Peter didn't return by dinnertime, Fannie was concerned but calm. He still had not returned when her caregiver helped put on her nightgown and get Fannie into bed. *Maybe he really did drive to Las Vegas. If so, he could be gone for a couple of days,* thought Fannie. Her sleep medicine kicked in and she fell into a troubled sleep.

The next morning, Fannie awoke to someone gently waking her. Her first thought was *Peter must be back,* but gentle was not Peter's style. "Fannie, wake up sweetheart. Open your eyes." Was she dreaming? "Come on, Fannie, open your eyes. It's Patsy." As she looked out of her half-opened eyes, she saw Patsy and Ms. Jackson standing over her.

Patsy leaned in and said, "Let me help you sit up, Fannie."

"Wha ... what's wrong?" asked Fannie as Patsy lifted her legs carefully, placing her feet on the floor.

"We have something we need to talk about," Susan replied softly. "Now don't worry, just sit up and get your bearings."

Patsy put a robe around Fannie's shoulders to ward off the morning chill. After that, Patsy helped her into her wheelchair, bathed her face with a warm washcloth, and ran a comb through her thinning hair. As Fannie was wheeled into the living room she again asked, "What's wrong?"

Patsy held Fannie's hand as Susan began. "Fannie, there was an accident. It seems Peter lost control of his car and went over a cliff on the coast road." Fannie sat there and stared ahead, not responding to Susan at all. Susan continued, "I called your daughter and she's on her way."

"Accident?" said Fannie. "An accident. How many times have I told him not to drive? Was he hurt?" Silent tears now appeared on her cheeks.

"Yes, Fannie, he was," Susan said hesitantly. She explained that the police said it was a very steep cliff and Peter didn't have much of a chance of surviving the impact. "Peter was gone by the time the police arrived, Fannie. I'm so sorry."

"Gone? You mean dead? Peter's dead?" sobbed Fannie.

Patsy put her arm around Fannie. "Oh Fannie, I'm so sorry." Patsy hugged her as Fannie slowly rocked back and forth. "It's going to be all right, sweetie. It's going to be all right."

Susan told Patsy that she had called Dr. Neil to come and give Fannie a sedative if needed. She suggested that Patsy stay with Fannie while she went downstairs to wait for Dr. Neil.

When the doctor arrived, Susan escorted him to

Fannie's room. He overheard Fannie talking to Patsy. "Why? Why, Patsy? Why did I let him leave? I knew he'd get right in that car and I knew he shouldn't be driving. It's all my fault."

Patsy stood up when she saw Dr. Neil come in. "Dr. Neil, she's very upset. She keeps saying that this is her fault. Nothing I say seems to convince her otherwise."

Dr. Neil moved in and took Fannie's hand in his. "Fannie, I'm very sorry to hear about your loss. We tend to blame ourselves when bad things happen to those we love, but the truth is we don't have control over everything. Sometimes accidents are just that – accidents. I'm going to give you something to settle your mind and help you sleep. Don't try to fight it, right now you need to rest. Patsy will stay with you until your daughter arrives."

Fannie was already getting drowsy when Dr. Neil turned to Patsy. "She should sleep until her daughter gets here. She needs time to ease the pain, the hurt and her guilt, however misplaced it may be."

Dr. Neil passed Susan's office on his way out and tapped on the door. She looked up and motioned for him to come in. "How are you doing?" he asked.

"I'm a little shaken up."

"Understandable. Mr. Gerrick passed in a pretty tragic way."

"Yes," Susan said, "but it's more than just that. Peter Gerrick is dead and I wished it on him. I *wanted* him gone, for Fannie's sake as well as my own. He was unpleasant and treated everyone terribly, but now that he's gone, she isn't any better off at all. She's hurting and she's in pain."

"Susan, you didn't drive his car off the cliff. Fannie will be fine eventually. Right now she's feeling the same guilt you are but a hundred times worse. Just do what you always do – take care of her."

Susan covered her eyes and shook her head. *I haven't taken care of any of the people in my life.* "He was a bastard, but she loved him," she murmured.

Dr. Neil touched her arm. "Most of the time, love is like a warm cocoon. But every once in a while, love is like bands of steel that set you free when broken. The bands have been broken. Fannie will be all right."

Word of Peter's death spread quickly around Balboa Shores. Sarah stayed quietly in her room. She meditated on peace for Fannie and prayed for Peter's soul. Catherine was indifferent. "He was old, old people die." Olga had mixed emotions. She

181

never liked the man but certainly didn't wish him dead. Miss Millie expressed her concern for Fannie. "Oh, the poor little bird." Maisie went around singing "Ding, dong, the witch is dead." Alletta mourned the passing of yet another man and the addition of another widow. Beatrice thought he shouldn't have been out there driving at all. Harry tried consoling everyone by hugging and cuddling. Delbert smiled as silent tears ran down his cheeks.

* * *

The police notified Peter's children about the circumstances surrounding his death. Fannie's daughter, Alice, called Peter's son to talk about funeral arrangements. His response was without emotion. "This is a surprise, but not entirely unexpected. My father expressed a desire to be cremated. Whatever service Fannie wants to have is fine with me. However, I won't be able to attend. I'll call you back with the address of the cemetery where the funeral home should send his ashes. He wanted to be interred beside his first wife, my mother."

Peter's daughter was a little more sensitive. "The three of us, at my brother's insistence, made prepaid cremation arrangements on our last visit for

Dad's birthday. Just keep the service simple and let me know the date. I'll be there."

The next day, Susan and Patsy took Fannie and her daughter to the healing garden courtyard to discuss plans for Peter's service. Patsy had a notepad to take notes. Susan began, "If we hold the service on a Sunday afternoon, we can ask the chaplain who comes in the morning to stay and conduct the service."

"That would be fine, Mom, don't you think?" Fannie had her eyes closed, listening to the birds' soft chatter.

Patsy sensed that Fannie just wanted to bask in the serenity of the healing garden for a bit. "It will be just your family, Peter's daughter, and a few friends and acquaintances. The chaplain could read a scripture and give a benediction. Harry has offered to sing. After that, we come out here to the garden and release balloons as a farewell."

Tears quietly escaped Fannie's eyes. "That sounds lovely, Patsy. My daughter Alice has been such a help. I don't know what I'd do without her."

"We'll also provide some refreshments after the balloon ceremony for those that want to stay and share memories with you," added Susan.

Alice spoke next. "Mom, how about next Sunday? Or would you prefer another day?"

"Sunday will do. Any day is fine. It doesn't make a difference." She paused. "He's gone. Peter's actually gone." Patsy and Alice went to check with the cook about refreshments and Susan went to her office to call the chaplain.

CHAPTER 29

The sun broke through the clouds to shine on Peter's memorial the following Sunday. Susan Jackson stood at the Great Room entrance, welcoming everyone as they arrived. Fannie sat in the front row of chairs flanked by her daughters and Peter's daughter. Patsy was pleasantly surprised to see Casey Howell sitting with his father, and also surprised to feel her heart race. *He looks pretty amazing in that suit.*

The minister began with a prayer and said a few words meant to comfort those in attendance. He then opened the microphone to the audience to share their memories of Peter. Several people spoke of their business relationship with Peter, but few talked about any sort of friendship. After everyone had the chance to speak, Susan motioned to Harry that it was time for his solo. He had decided to sing *When Irish Eyes are Smiling*. Patsy wondered *why in the world would he choose that song? Gerrick certainly isn't an Irish name.* But Fannie had said whatever Harry wanted to sing was fine. Looking over, Patsy saw Fannie dab at her eyes with a white handkerchief edged in pale pink crochet, a gift from Olga.

At the conclusion of the song, Susan suggested

that everyone gather in the rose garden to release the balloons. She and Patsy handed a balloon to each person as they passed through the door. Giving Casey a balloon, Patsy's hand brushed his. She definitely felt a spark. *Or was it just the balloon?* Patsy was certain he had felt it too. He smiled as he thanked her.

Outside, in her frail voice, Fannie thanked everyone for coming. She invited them to let their balloons go at the count of three as a final goodbye to Peter. Fannie's voice softened to little more than a whisper. "Peter, rest in peace. One, two, three." All was quiet as the group watched the graceful assembly of white balloons slowly ascend and drift away. Susan spoke. "Fannie would like to invite each of you to have some refreshments in the Activities Room."

As people milled around, Casey walked over to Patsy. "The balloons were a thoughtful gesture. Were they your idea?"

"Yes. It's sort of a Balboa Shores tradition. It was nice of you to come to hear your father sing."

"Can't pass up a chance to hear my dear old dad belt one out." He paused. "And I wanted to see you."

The residents were scattering now. "Any particular reason?" asked Patsy.

Casey put his hands on her shoulders and smiled. "I have tickets to *Phantom of the Opera* later this month and I was hoping you would accompany me."

"I've heard the music from *Phantom* but I've never seen it. The music is so beautiful – hauntingly beautiful. Yes, I'd love to see it."

"With me?"

"Of course with you!" She smiled. "You asked me, didn't you?"

"It's a date, then?"

"Yes, it's a date."

* * *

Patsy was whistling when she arrived at work Monday morning. Catherine was sitting in the foyer with her ever-present portrait and satchel. Patsy was just leaving the staff room, ready to distract Catherine, when the distress buzzer for Miss Millie's apartment went off. Patsy turned and ran up the stairs.

"Miss Millie," she called as she opened the door to 241.

"I'm in here," Miss Millie answered from the bathroom. As Patsy pushed open the door to the bathroom, she could see Miss Millie seated on the commode, her feathered pink robe pooling onto the floor, and her hair wrapped in the bandana she wore at night to keep her set fresh. The bathroom looked like mischievous children had splattered the counter and walls with globs of glue. Miss Millie sobbed, "I can't make the stupid thing work. I can't make it work!"

Patsy looked around and, spotting nothing obvious, turned back to Miss Millie. "Make what work? What happened here?"

Miss Millie wiped her eyes with toilet tissue and pointed to the trash can next to the sink. Inside, humming away, lay a new aqua and white battery-powered toothbrush. The bristles vibrated against the side of the trash can with a pulsating sound. "My daughter got it for me and now it's ruined, worthless."

Giving the bathroom a sweeping gesture with her hand, Patsy asked, "How did all this happen?"

Miss Millie answered between sobs. "I put the toothpaste on the brush ... and pressed the button ... and the toothpaste ... went flying all over. I kept trying, but it just kept flying off the brush, onto the walls, again and again and again."

Patsy laughed. She couldn't help herself. "Miss Millie, Miss Millie, and here I thought you were becoming an octogenarian Jackson Pollock!"

Miss Millie looked up from her damp wad of toilet paper. "Jackson who?"

"Jackson Pollock. He was an artist who sloshed paint all over the place and called it art," Patsy said. "Let's see if we can retrieve the toothbrush and I can show you how to use it without painting the walls." She cleaned the brush under the hot water tap while explaining to Miss Millie that she needed to put the brush in her mouth before turning it on. "See, then when the toothpaste starts flying, it will be in your mouth and you can just continue brushing your teeth."

Clapping her hands down flat on her lap, she looked at Patsy with amazement. "Patsy, are you really that smart or am I really that dumb?"

"Neither, Miss Millie. But I do know a few useful things, that's all. Now why don't you try it again?" She stood and watched as Miss Millie completed the procedure flawlessly.

"That was easy," sighed Miss Millie. "I was afraid I was becoming incapable of doing even the simplest things for myself."

"I hope you see that you're quite capable, Miss Millie. I'll call housekeeping to come and clean this bathroom. Don't worry, I'll explain what happened so you won't have to go into the story again. In the meantime, why don't you sit down and read or do something that will calm your nerves? And just remember: all's well that ends well."

Later that afternoon, Susan called Patsy into her office. "I understand the resident in 241 used her distress button for a non-emergency."

"It was an emergency to her. She was in a very emotional state."

"An emotional state over an electric toothbrush hardly qualifies as an emergency, Patsy. Please explain to her again what she *is* and *is not* allowed to use the distress button for. And tell her if she doesn't want to be considered an emergent risk, which could cost her more care points, it mustn't happen again. I'll need to put this incident into her file. That's all, Patsy."

Bitch, thought Patsy.

CHAPTER 30

It was a chilly evening and Patsy had a small fire going in the fireplace when Casey arrived for their date to *Phantom*. She opened the door wearing her second new outfit in the last month. It made her feel flirty if not outright seductive.

"You look beautiful tonight," Casey said, lifting her hand in the air and twirling her around. Smiling, Patsy said, "Thank you. You look smashing yourself. Would you like a drink? I don't have a large selection, but I've got white wine and some bourbon."

"Bourbon sounds perfect." Sinatra played softly in the background as Casey sat down and eyed the apartment. "You have a lovely home. It looks like you. Very warm and cozy."

"Thanks," Patsy said, handing him his drink. "It's mostly old pieces that I've refinished." She sat on the couch next to him.

Casey took a sip as his eyes perused the room. He put down his drink and pointed to a photograph. "Is that your husband?"

Patsy went to the picture and brought it over to the couch. "Yes, this was taken when Bud first enlisted and got his full uniform. It was quite a big day for us."

"He was in the Marines, right?"

"Right. For seven years. His last tour was Iraq. He's been gone three years now."

Casey picked up the picture. "He looks just as you described him, an all-American boy."

"He was special. Really, the first and only man in my life."

Casey put down the picture and looked at Patsy. "I hope I'm in the running to be the second."

"Casey Howell, I'll be straight with you. The hot-headed jerk I met back in October wouldn't stand a chance, but the new and improved Casey might just have a shot. Although I have to admit," Patsy said, her eyes shyly checking him out, "I always liked the packaging."

Casey leaned in for a kiss. Patsy closed her eyes and smiled, drinking in the sweet taste of bourbon on his lips.

A contented Patsy slowly opened her eyes. "We'd better get going. Don't want to be late for our dinner reservations or the play." Reluctantly, they both stood up.

The restaurant was fancier than Patsy was used to, but she felt comfortable with Casey by her side. "Escargot!" she exclaimed as she browsed the menu. "I've heard of it but never had it."

A smile came to Casey's face. "Well then, will

you be adventurous and try it?"

Patsy wrinkled her nose. "I don't know if I could actually eat a snail."

"They're delicious," Casey assured her. "They mostly taste like butter and garlic. You usually only get six to a plate. What if I get one as an appetizer and we share it? How does that sound?"

"Sounds possible," teased Patsy.

A wonderful smell of garlic and butter engulfed their table when the escargot arrived. Six gunmetal gray shriveled … *things* sat in individual compartments on the plate. *Like deviled eggs, but much smaller,* thought Patsy. They were swimming in butter, garnished with some green sprinkles, and around the platter were tiny toast points.

"If I could just close my eyes and smell them, I'd be happy."

Casey patted her hand. "You'd be much happier if you closed your eyes and let me pop one into your mouth. We'll follow it with a small piece of bread soaked in the garlic butter."

Feeling adventurous, Patsy closed her eyes, opened her mouth, and felt her tongue being teased with the tiny mollusks. She chewed and swallowed and, surprising even herself, smiled. The next bite was so delicious she almost wanted to stop the tasting game and eat the whole order herself.

Instead, she opened her eyes and found herself looking straight into Casey's baby blues. "Your turn now," Patsy murmured, piercing an escargot with the tiny hors d'oeuvre fork. Casey obediently closed his eyes and opened his mouth.

The theater was crowded and noisy as they took their seats. They had to huddle close to each other with their heads together to be heard. As the lights went down and the orchestra began to play, Casey interlocked his fingers with Patsy's.

Patsy though the music and the scenery were breathtaking in equal measure. She thought she might dissolve into tears at the beauty of the underground scene with all the candles. Casey squeezed her hand and she held it together. "I *love* this music," Patsy exclaimed at intermission. Patsy was impressed when Casey stood in a long line to buy the soundtrack for her. *I can't imagine the old Casey ever doing that,* she thought.

Afterward, Casey invited Patsy to his house to listen to the CD and have a glass of wine. They were relaxing on the sofa, their shoes off, Patsy curled up with her back to his chest. Casey's arms held her close. Patsy's voice was dreamy as she whispered, "Thank you for the beautiful evening and for this fantastic CD." She turned her head and kissed him softly.

Casey, nuzzling her hair, kissed her back. Patsy felt her body beginning to tingle. She had all but forgotten this sensation. Her body turned to his as her reserve melted into an eager response.

Casey was a tender and practiced lover. Patsy was surprised at her own lovemaking. She had always been more submissive with Bud, but now she felt the great power of her sexuality.

That night their lovemaking went from short and fast, to long and sweet. Their needs were both satisfied and yet left them wanting more.

In the morning Patsy awoke to the sound of Casey making breakfast. She put on a shirt from his closet and padded into the kitchen.

Casey looked up from the stove. "Good morning," he smiled.

Patsy blushed. "Good morning to you, too."

Casey wrapped his arms around her. She buried her head in his chest. "Thank you for letting me into your life. Not just for the sex, but thanks for letting me in for that, too." Patsy laughed and Casey picked her up and hugged her while turning in circles. "Your attire is becoming. Are you ready for breakfast?"

"Starving."

After they ate, Casey showed Patsy around his house. The bedroom had French doors that opened onto a small enclosed brick patio and garden. A path through the garden led to a pool and steaming spa. Across was another patio with french doors that led back into the living room. "It's beautiful," said Patsy. "How do you keep up with all the work? Everything looks immaculate."

"I have a gardener who helps out, but even then I don't get much time to enjoy just being home. And I can't remember the last time I used the spa."

"I'd use it all the time if I had all this," said Patsy. "In fact, let's do it now!" She shed the shirt and slipped into the spa. Aroused by her spontaneity, Casey followed.

After Casey dropped Patsy at her house on Sunday evening, she felt alone. It was different from the loneliness she'd been living with for the past three years. She missed the laughing, the kissing, the touching, the sex. She missed Casey. She dreamed about how satisfying a life with him would be.

CHAPTER 31
FEBRUARY

Every winter the Junior League sponsored an outdoor ice skating rink as a fundraiser for the Children's Hospital. Many of the Balboa Shores residents had grown up skating on lakes or ponds, so Patsy planned a trip to watch the skaters – from the warmth of a covered veranda. It wasn't a lake nor a pond, just an artificial surface covered with ice. The trip would get everyone out into the crisp fresh air and, Patsy hoped, chase away the winter blahs.

Harry had asked Casey to come along and he had agreed. Patsy welcomed the chance to spend time with Casey.

Patsy and the staff made sure everyone was dressed warmly. A white picket fence circled the rink and music filled the air. Outside the fence, tables surrounded the area where observers could sit and watch while butane heaters kept them warm. The Junior League provided hot chocolate and cookies. Patsy helped deliver the snacks.

"How are you doing, Delbert?" asked Patsy, setting a cup of hot chocolate in front of him.

"I'm doin' fine, even if it is colder than an outhouse in a snowstorm." Delbert was in a good mood. "It was so cold where I grew up, they had to sell milk by the pound." Patsy rolled her eyes at a story she had heard countless times before and bent down to pet Jack, who was busy lapping up a puddle of spilled hot chocolate.

Casey sat between his father and Patsy. "Some of those skaters look professional, but others look like they have three left feet," he observed.

Patsy took a sip of her hot chocolate. "The graceful ones have probably had many years of practice."

"Are you a skater, Patsy?"

"I did skate growing up. There's been no time for it in the last few years. How about you?"

"I've never tried it."

"That surprises me. You are quite the athlete, aren't you?"

Casey smiled. "I don't think ice skating and baseball pull from the same skill set. Why don't we try it together? You can hold me up if I start to fall."

"If I didn't have this crew with me," said Patsy, indicating the group of elderly residents sitting around them, "I might take you up on that. It would either be fun or a complete disaster."

"Let's do it! We can come back tonight and you can teach me."

Patsy hadn't been ice skating for years. The look

she gave Casey was doubtful.

"Come on, it'll be fun," Casey coaxed. "Don't make me beg. I will, but it won't be pretty."

"I wouldn't rely on me holding you up if I were you."

"Is that a yes?"

"It's a yes."

* * *

The atmosphere at the skating rink that night was magical, a fairyland brought to life. Twinkling blue-tinted icicles and snowflakes hung above the skaters, turning them into shimmering, dancing sprites. After lacing up their skates, Patsy pulled Casey out onto the ice. He hesitated. "I don't think I'm ready to let go of the railing just yet. Why don't you go first and show me what to do?"

Patsy skated off and was surprised to find herself whirling around the rink with ease. She took a second lap and did some turns and even skated backwards for a few seconds. She skated back over to Casey and reached for his hand. "Come on, let's try it together now. I'll hold your hand."

"What if I fall down? Or worse, what if I fall on you?"

"Hey mister, this was your idea. Don't wimp out

on me now!"

Casey took her hand and they negotiated the rink three times before sitting down to rest.

"Thanks for suggesting this, Casey. I'm having a lot of fun," said Patsy. Her hair was damp and curling in ringlets around her flushed cheeks. The lights reflected in her eyes, making them an even deeper blue.

"I've never had such a good time making a complete fool out of myself," replied Casey. "Hey, I'm starting to get hungry. Shall we get something to eat?"

"Pizza sounds good," said Patsy, blowing into her mittened hands. They walked down the street to the Hot Italian Pizzeria on 21st and Mission.

"What kind of pizza do you like?" Casey asked. "They have some very unique combinations here. How do you feel about trying to prosciutto and fig with balsamic vinegar?"

Patsy smiled. Even with her nose bright red from the cold, Casey thought she looked charming. "This seems to be a night for new experiences," she said.

They settled down with their food and beer and, for a few minutes, neither spoke as they greedily devoured the surprisingly delicious pizza.

"Wow! I think I may have found my new favorite pizza," Patsy said, her eyes opening wide. "A good choice, Casey."

Wiping his mouth with a napkin, Casey asked Patsy how she thought his father was doing. She told him the truth, that Harry was becoming more forgetful and that she often had to remind him that they were just good friends and nothing more. Casey told her he'd noticed Harry had become less energetic and rarely mentioned his "darlin" these days, but always spoke of Patsy with the utmost respect.

"Alletta seems to give him a good deal of attention," Casey said offhandedly.

"Alletta is quite the flirt, but she's harmless enough," Patsy assured him. "That's enough work talk for tonight. I'm getting cold. I think it might be time to call it a night."

They walked back to the car hand in hand, enjoying the music from the skating rink and each other. When they pulled up in front of Patsy's house, Patsy said good night and again told him what a good time she had had.

"Good night, Patsy." Casey leaned over and gave her a quick, soft kiss. She hopped out and quickly ran to her door, looking back over her shoulder to give him a short wave before unlocking the door and going inside.

Later, Patsy lay on her bed in one of Bud's old

flannel shirts, the kiss still lingering on her lips. She closed her eyes and heard Bud's sweet voice. *It's time you let go of me. You have so much love to give and your whole life ahead of you. Go out there and live it.*

Tears came to her eyes. *I never thought I'd have to live without you, Bud.* She waited for him to speak again, but the room remained silent.

CHAPTER 32

Patsy couldn't stop grinning. In fact, she was beaming. "Good morning, Catherine! What a beautiful day." Patsy was rewarded with a silent stare. "Come on, Catherine, let's go do something fun." Patsy took Catherine by the hands and pulled her out of the big chair by the entrance.

Patsy led Catherine to the Activities Room where Judith, one of Balboa Shores' long-time caregivers, sat with a box of grocery items. The game she was starting was a homegrown version of *The Price is Right*. Judith held up a can of tuna and a can of green beans. She asked the group, "Which one do you think costs more?" Several shouted "the tuna!" while one or two declared "the beans!" She wrote the word "tuna" and then checked the price written on the bottom of the can. $1.69 went next to the word in big black numbers. Then, checking the bottom of the can of beans, she wrote "green beans $0.79." The residents who had guessed correctly smiled and nodded their triumphant approval.

Next, Judith held up a pair of socks and a pair of slippers. As if on cue, Fannie burst into tears. Fannie was still grieving over Peter's death. As Fannie sobbed, Patsy took her chair over next to Fannie's and put her arm around her. "Fannie, what's wrong?" she asked.

"Those slipper socks were the last thing Peter bought before he died."

Patsy remembered how nasty Peter had been at the last bingo auction. She had truly disliked Peter Gerrick, but she couldn't help but feel sorry for Fannie's loss. She took Fannie back to her room and fixed her a cup of tea.

Maisie was also having a difficult day. Apparently, this morning before Patsy arrived, Judith went in to wake her and give Maisie her medication. She noticed the bedroom carpet was soggy wet. When Judith asked her about it, Maisie said simply, "I was watering my flowers. Aren't they beautiful?" Then she opened up her closet and showed the caregiver her colorful dance shoes, all lined up in a row, soaking wet and completely ruined. Patsy asked to talk to Susan Jackson about Maisie. By four o'clock, it was hard to keep smiling. Patsy was exhausted. Thank goodness she was having dinner with Casey tonight.

* * *

At home, she changed into jeans and a sweater and picked up her car keys to head out. Casey was cooking dinner at his house. Patsy was locking her front door when she thought *I might be staying for more than dinner* and went back inside to get her toothbrush and a change of clothes.

Casey welcomed her with a soft, warm kiss. Her head rested against his chest and she let out a long, satisfied, tired sigh.

"Hard day today?" asked Casey.

"Yes. I'm really looking forward to a relaxing dinner."

"That's exactly what I have planned. Let me get you a drink and you can tell me about your day."

Patsy sat at the kitchen counter with a glass of red wine while Casey tossed a salad to go with the lasagna. She told him first how Fannie had dissolved into tears over a pair of slipper socks.

"You remember me telling you about Maisie, the one who prances around in her old dancing shoes?" Patsy proceeded to tell Casey the story of Maisie and her shoe garden.

"When I met with Susan late this afternoon, she decided it was time for Maisie to be placed in the Alzheimer's Unit. She'll be moved tomorrow and she probably won't even notice. I'll miss her, but realistically she probably won't miss any of us. She was a chorus girl, you know, and had pictures of her performances all over her apartment. Those shoes were an important part of her life. Now she doesn't recognize them and doesn't care about them."

"She must care about them if she's watering them so much," Casey teased.

"Oh Casey, it's just so sad. I do think that moving her to the Alzheimer's Unit is the right thing to do. But that doesn't make it any easier."

Carrying the salad to the table, Casey said, "You know, we're all going to get old. Hopefully our bodies give out before our minds, but there's no guarantee of that. You've given all your residents so much kindness and love. You're going to have to trust that the people who run the Alzheimer's Unit will do the same."

Patsy set her wine down on the table. "When our residents get to that stage, they can only be given a series of good moments, but not memories that will stick. I hope she has enough good memories from the past to keep her content." Patsy tasted the salad. "Delicious. Sliced pears and walnuts, what a lovely touch."

Sitting on the couch after dinner, Casey said, "Tell me about your childhood. I bet you were a handful growing up."

"If you want to know the truth, my childhood was pretty idyllic. I was an only child and my daddy's little tomboy. I followed him around our farm and imitated everything he did. He let me help him mend gates, feed oats to the horses from a bucket, dig up radishes, little things like that. Sometimes I got to ride on the tractor with him. He never made me feel like I was a nuisance, unlike my mother."

"Nuisance?" Casey asked. "How so?"

"Mom was a good cook and had her hands full feeding a bunch of hungry farmhands. She didn't try to make me into Susie Homemaker. I think she knew there was no hope for me in that arena and I'm sure she didn't need nor want me underfoot in the kitchen. I liked to play outside. I liked to climb trees, chase rabbits, ride bareback and skip stones across our pond. I never played with dolls or helped Mom cook. I had to clean my room and help with chores inside, but I didn't like it and was always finding an excuse to stay out until the sun went down. I think It made my mother a little jealous that I was so close to my dad."

"I don't see a tomboy now. When did you grow out of that phase?"

"I didn't really start to notice boys until high school. I was a cheerleader." Casey grinned. Patsy continued, "I only became a cheerleader because it was the only extracurricular sport for girls. I loved the jumping and making pyramids. It wasn't long before boys started to notice me and I didn't mind too much."

"When did you get your first kiss?"

"My first kiss was from Bud. I was a sophomore. He sure made my hormones start raging. I ended up marrying him right after graduation." Patsy sighed, as though she had told her whole story in one breath. "Now it's your turn. Tell me all about little Casey."

Casey laughed softly. "Well, I didn't grow up on a farm. I'm a city boy. Instead of farm chores I went out and got in trouble."

Patsy punched him playfully. "Come on, be serious."

"I mean it. I was even thrown in juvenile hall for a short stretch."

Patsy's eyes widened and she covered her mouth with her hand. "What did you do?"

"I borrowed a car – without permission. But that was when I was a teenager. I grew up in the San Bernardino Valley, playing t-ball, little league, swimming at the community pool and riding my bike with my friends. By the time I turned sixteen, my father had started his construction business and put me to work learning the building trade."

"Did you finish high school?"

"Oh yes. I wouldn't have been allowed to drop out of school. I worked for him after school and on weekends to earn extra money. I got tired of all work and no play though. I thought I was so grown-up. I was cool, and I wanted some fun. I bought a secondhand car and started drinking on weekends with my friends. I worked on my car and cruised around town a lot, looking for trouble."

Patsy smiled. "So, if you had your own car, why did you take someone else's?"

"For excitement. One night we had a few beers and saw my neighbor park his BMW in the parking lot of a bar. I got it in my head that I deserved a nicer car. So we hot wired the car and took a joy ride to the next town over. The police, of course, considered it stolen, and I was sentenced to three months in juvie and probation. It probably would have been just probation, but my dad told the judge that he thought I needed some jail time to think about things. That's how hard-assed my dad was in those days. But, looking back, it was probably the best thing that happened to me."

"Why?"

"It got me to go to college."

"What? How did going to jail get you to go to college?"

"About a month in juvie, my dad said he could get his lawyer to petition the judge for an early release. All he needed would be proof that I intended to enroll in college. It would show the court that I intended to settle down and get my life back on track. It took me another week of bad food and boredom to consent to filling out the college application. Having the application in hand, along with the fact that this was my one and only offense, the judge took my sentence under consideration and I was out in a few days. At college I studied hard enough to keep me out of trouble, and I managed to have a little fun too. I got a B.A. In business and then returned to work for my father."

"And what about your mother? What was she like?"

"Long-suffering and believe me, she let you know it. She turned a blind eye to dad's indiscretions. She enjoyed all the perks available to the wife of a successful contractor. She let Dad deal with me for the most part. My sister Carolyn was her favorite. Unlike your mom, she insisted my sister master all the things a wife and good hostess is supposed to know. My sister ended up eloping at the age of twenty."

"Where does she live now?"

"She lives in New York, but we talk often. She loved our mom and tolerated our dad. She was the one who nursed our mom when Mom was diagnosed with cancer. After Mom died, she had a bit of a breakdown and couldn't take care of Dad, so

I stepped in and moved him close to me. I'm responsible for his well-being and you know how touchy I can get over that."

Patsy brushed some hair from his forehead. "Yes, I know, and it took me some time to see how loving and caring you really are." They sat looking into the fireplace, entwined in comfortable silence.

CHAPTER 33
APRIL

Catherine and Sarah sat warm and cozy in the living room as rain continued to fall outside, encouraging the spring grass to sprout. "Will this rain ever end?" moaned Catherine, eying the water running down the french doors. Getting no response, Catherine turned to Sarah. Seeing her eyes closed and her head leaning forward to her chest, Catherine shook Sarah.

"Wake up! Sarah, wake up." Sarah remained unresponsive. "Fine company *you* are," barked Catherine as she stood up and started to walk toward her room. Passing Patsy in the hallway, Catherine told her that Sarah had fallen asleep in the living room and someone needed to wake her up.

"Let's wake her up together," Patsy suggested.

"I already tried. She won't wake up for me. She can be stubborn as a mule." Still, Catherine followed Patsy back to the living room. Seeing the slumped Sarah, Patsy rushed to check her pulse, then paged the front desk.

"Call 911. I'm in the living room with Sarah. Send the nurse."

Agitated, Catherine kept repeating, "She's just

asleep. *Wake up, Sarah! Wake up.*" The nurse arrived shortly and asked Catherine to leave the room. Gently, Patsy took Catherine by the arm and led her out of the living room. "She'll be all right, Catherine. The nurse will help Sarah." Catherine's eyes never left her friend, as she and Patsy turned the corner and went into the Activities Room.

"Let's watch the *Price is Right.* You like that show, don't you?"

"Yes, but I want Sarah to come watch with us."

"She will. Soon," assured Patsy. She kept Catherine in the Activities Room and turned up the volume when she heard the sirens approaching. The paramedics quickly loaded Sarah into the ambulance. Worried but trying not to show it, Patsy helped Catherine back to her room and into bed for a nap.

* * *

Sarah was taken to the Sisters of Mercy Hospital, where ER doctors determined that she had suffered a severe heart attack. Her end-of-life directive made it clear she did not want any heroic actions performed to prolong her life. That evening, she remained in critical condition in the ICU.

Knowing that Sarah likely did not have long to

live, Susan Jackson placed a call to Kavi Sinn. He had just returned to India from Balboa Shores a little over a month ago. When told that Sarah's condition was listed as day to day, he said he would be on the next flight out of Allahabad.

Kavi Sinn arrived two days later, exhausted from jet lag but determined to see Sarah. He ignored Ms. Jackson's advice to rest a while and went straight to the hospital. Dr. Neil told him it was only a matter of time, maybe hours, before Sarah would pass. Her systems were shutting down.

"Can I talk to her?" he asked.

"Of course. Hearing is one of the last senses to shut down, so we do think she can hear you. But she won't be able to respond," said Dr. Neil.

"I don't need her to talk. I just want to let her know that I'm here. Maybe she won't be so afraid." Kavi Sinn entered the room and stood by Sarah's bed. Within an instant, he was once again that little boy who cried for help at the river and was given such love from a young girl only twice his age. He took her hand and kissed it.

"*Memsaab*, I'm here. Kavi is here." He leaned over and kissed her on the forehead. Sarah's eyes remained shut; she looked serene. "How peaceful and sweet you look. If you are ready to leave this world and go home, it will cause me pain, but I know that even better things await you in your next life."

Struggling to maintain composure, Kavi continued. "Talk it over with your God tonight and know that you have been and still are much loved." He stayed holding her hands for a few minutes longer, then quietly left the room.

Three days passed, and every day Kavi Sinn came to the hospital and held Sarah's hand and brushed the hair from her forehead. Everyone at Balboa Shores was asking about Sarah. When would she be allowed to have visitors? When was she coming back? Patsy didn't know how to answer.

Sarah never regained consciousness, and died peacefully five days later.

Patsy made an effort to personally notify those close to Sarah of her passing. On the mantel in the living room, a brief notice was placed in the appointed gilded frame. Soon everyone knew. Strangely, Catherine was the person the residents were worried about. What would she do without her little Sarah to lead around? Who would listen to her complaints with such patience? Who would she boss around? Poor, poor Catherine.

* * *

The memorial for Sarah was held in the Great

Room by the fireplace. Harry sang his standard *When Irish Eyes are Smiling.* Kavi Sinn, looking distinguished with his graying temples and expensive pinstriped suit, took the podium and began to speak.

"It was a long time ago, when I was just a boy, that I first met Mata Sarah. That's what we called her, *Mata*, Mother, because of her dedication and loving care to the sick, despised and lonely. She found me scared and hurt by the side of the river, and she took me to her mission. Her quick thinking saved my foot from amputation. Sarah Elizabeth Owen was one of the strongest influences in my life. I am a better and more compassionate man today because of her love, friendship, and loyalty. You might have known her as a quiet meek soul, and she was; but in her prime, Sarah was a powerful and stubborn force for good, yet she never once lost her humility. I will always remember her humor, her intelligence, her compassion, and her cheerfulness in every situation. She will be long remembered, she will not be forgotten, as her spirit resides in the hearts of those she served in her beloved India."

Catherine displayed more emotion during the service than anyone thought her capable. She dabbed at her red eyes with a tissue. For several days, she roamed the halls of Balboa Shores, looking for Sarah. Not finding her, she would stop anyone who would listen and ask, "Where's Sarah? Have you seen Sarah?" Patsy sat Catherine down and explained that it was normal for her to miss Sarah, but that she had died, was gone for good and would not be coming back. Catherine looked sternly at Patsy. "I didn't say I missed her, I simply asked where she is. I suppose she went on a trip and didn't tell me, as usual." Pasty waked away slowly, worrying that Catherine's dementia was getting worse day by day.

CHAPTER 34

Patsy entered Balboa Shores on a bright April morning to see Catherine sitting in the foyer, her ever-present satchel and portrait leaning against the wall next to her. Patsy gently took her hand and tried to coax Catherine from the chair, but Catherine resisted and, with unusual strength, pulled her arm away. Patsy signed and went to the Activities Room. Knowing Catherine's fondness for game shows, she flipped on the large-screen TV, scrolled through the channels, and finding the big wheel, returned to the foyer.

Patsy squatted down and looked Catherine in the eye. "*Wheel of Fortune* is on, Catherine, and I'm stuck on the puzzle. Could you come help me figure it out?"

Catherine looked at her suspiciously. "Really? They're not that challenging."

"I know, but you're the best. I need your help."

Catherine rose from the chair in a graceful swoop and left her things behind as she followed Patsy to the Activities Room. With hardly a glance at the television screen, she declared her answer to the puzzle: "I know how the caged bird sings." It wasn't even close, but Patsy thanked her. As Catherine continued to watch *Wheel of Fortune*,

Patsy called for a caregiver to pick up Catherine's belongings and return them to her room.

After lunch, Catherine returned to her perch by the front door and observed everyone as they came and went. She nervously pinched the fabric of her skirt and twisted it into a circle with her fingers. Patsy asked her to come to arts and crafts.

"I can't. I'm waiting for Alejandro. He's coming to get me."

"I'm sure he'll wait for you, Catherine," Patsy said, guiding Catherine to the Activities Room.

Making the paper beads was difficult for the residents, and helping Delbert and the rest of the crew took most of Patsy's attention. Afterward, Patsy found Catherine had slipped out and was once again sitting in the foyer with her satchel and painting. Patsy sighed and turned away. *Just sit there, then, and don't bother anyone. Maybe Ms. Jackson will finally deal with you.*

Catherine did indeed sit there for the rest of the afternoon. At dinner a haggard-looking Catherine snapped at Olga, admonishing her to wipe her mouth and not to speak with food in it.

"Oh, shut up, you old hag," said Olga.

"Olga, please," said Miss Millie. "Catherine's probably mistaking you for Sarah. You can see how tired she looks. Catherine, why don't you go up to bed and get a good night's sleep? That'll do you good."

About eleven o'clock, Catherine awoke feeling fully rested. She'd had a wonderful dream about Alejandro. With his dark eyes and windblown hair, he was holding out his hand to her, his eyes begging her to come to him. *Of course,* she thought, *there must be some reason he can't come to me.* She would go to him.

Catherine got out of bed and hurriedly put her peasant skirt on over her pajamas. Pulling the cord on her gaucho hat tightly under her chin, she felt happy and excited. As she reached for the portrait on the wall, she noticed it was dark outside. *I'd better take a wrap; it looks chilly.* She grabbed the poncho that Sarah had knitted for her. *Sarah. Sarah will feel left out when she finds out I've gone to Spain without her. Sorry, Sarah, but this is a lover's tryst.*

She walked down the hall as quietly as she could. A thin line of light shone from under the closed staff room door. She could hear the second shift workers briefing the overnight staff before they left for the night. Without a peep, Catherine slipped out the front door unnoticed. Seeing lights in the distance to the north, she decided to walk toward them.

She reached the lighted street still carrying her satchel and painting. The load was becoming heavy and Catherine found herself breathing heavy. The flood of bright neon signs confused her. She sat down to rest at a bus stop. She had her eyes closed when a taxi pulled up. "Lady, do you need a ride? The buses don't run this late on week nights."

Mistaking the cab for one of her father's limos, her reply was curt. "I've been waiting for you." The driver got out and helped her put her things in the seat beside her.

"Where to?"

"Spain."

"Then you want the airport, right?" Nodding her head, Catherine sat back and again closed her eyes to rest.

"Where are you going in Spain?" No answer. She didn't feel like talking and it was her business, not his. "I've never been there myself. I hear the weather is great, but maybe a little too hot for me. What airline do you want?"

"Oh, any of them will be fine," Catherine said.

The taxi driver shook his head. "Okay then, I'll drop you off at the international terminal." He pulled up to the curb and jumped out to help her with her bags. Picking up her things, she thanked him and started to walk away. "Hey, lady, wait! You didn't pay me." Catherine kept walking.

"Hey, come back. You owe me money," he said as he caught up with her. Catherine stopped, turned, and glared at the driver.

"Do you know who I am, young man? I am Catherine Kingston Hughes. My father pays your salary!"

"No ma'am, I don't know any Mr. Hughes, and he sure doesn't pay my salary. I work for A&B Taxi Company."

"When I talk to my father, you may not work for *anyone* any more!" Catherine turned and started toward the terminal doors.

"Lady, I don't even know your father. I don't care about your pop, I just want my money. You owe me fifteen dollars."

As the automatic doors closed behind Catherine, the airport security guard urged the cab driver to move his vehicle. "Keep moving. This isn't a taxi stand, just drop off."

"But she didn't pay me."

"Take it up with the judge," said the security guard. "Move on, buddy."

Once inside, Catherine looked around and was quickly overwhelmed by the noise and the chaos. She went up to a man in line and asked, "Where do I go to get to Spain?" He ignored her. She approached another traveler and another. Finally, a sympathetic soul pointed to the escalator that led to the security checkpoint. Catherine went up the escalator and stood in line. Very tired now, she set her things down and tried to scoot them along with her feet as she progressed in line. Approaching the scanning machines, she was asked for her ID and boarding pass.

"I'm Catherine Kingston Hughes and I'm going to Spain."

"Ma'am, I need to see your ID and your boarding pass."

"I just *told* you who I am."

The line had come to a standstill. The agent asked Catherine to step to the side for a moment, then waved another security guard over to talk with her.

"Ma'am, don't you have an ID on you?" he asked.

Frustrated, Catherine replied, "I don't know. Just let me go."

"How about your boarding pass?" asked the man, gently taking hold of her arm.

"Let go of me! I just want to go to Spain." The guard let go of her arm and very patiently asked, "Do you think your ID might be in your bag?"

Catherine brightened. "Of course! That's where it

is."

"Great. Can you get it out for me, please?"

Catherine rummaged around in her satchel. "What am I looking for?"

"ID and boarding pass, ma'am."

"I can't seem to find them. Just let me go. I"m going to miss my plane."

"Sorry, ma'am, but I can't let you do that." Seeing that she was more than a little confused, he said, "Why don't we go to my office, have some tea, and see if we can sort this out?" The guard picked up her satchel and painting with one hand and placed the other on the small of her back, guiding Catherine to the security office.

As soon as Catherine sat down in the comfortable armchair, her exhaustion took over. She closed her eyes and was soon asleep. The security guard went through her satchel and, finding no identification, picked up the phone and called the city police.

"Good evening, officer. My name is Charles Harlan and I'm a security guard at the airport. We have an older Caucasian female in custody who seems to be mentally disturbed. She doesn't look like she's homeless, but she is dressed rather flamboyantly. She has clothes on over her pajamas and she doesn't have any identification on her.

She's carrying just one small cloth bag and a large oil painting. She's very disoriented and was a trifle combative until she fell asleep. Yes, she's asleep now. Do you want to come and get her? Yes, officer, I'll just let her rest until you arrive."

* * *

The next morning Patsy was surprised to see Susan Jackson already in her office when she arrived at six o'clock. Patsy waved and Susan motioned for her to come in.

"I've been here almost all night," Susan said, stifling a yawn.

Patsy could see the stress in her face. "What is it? What happened?"

Susan looked at Patsy with weary eyes. "Catherine disappeared last night." A sickening feeling started to grow in the pit of Patsy's stomach. "Her disappearance was discovered around midnight when Judy did a bed check. She's back here now and sleeping, thank God, but it's been a traumatic few hours. We checked the entire place to be sure she hadn't fallen or ended up in someone else's bedroom. When Judy noticed Catherine's satchel and painting were also gone, she called me."

"Oh my goodness. Did you call the police?"

"I did. The police immediately put out an APB for a missing person."

"Don't they have to wait forty-eight hours to declare someone missing?" asked Patsy.

"Not if the person is in a memory or Alzheimer's facility," Susan explained. "By that time, the senior might be in real trouble. No, they get on it right away. I also called several taxi companies and asked them to check their logs to see if any of their drivers were dispatched here in the middle of the night. None had any record of it. I sent Judy out in the car to search the neighborhood street by street. About an hour after she left, I got a call back from the police department saying a woman fitting Catherine's description was found at the airport. She was trying to get on a plane to Spain but didn't have a ticket or any sort of identification with her." Susan rested her elbows on her desk and continued. "Evidently, Catherine was making quite a fuss. They took her downtown and kept her until Judy and I went to pick her up. We just got back about an hour ago, and I'm exhausted now so I'm going home for a few hours to rest. Please keep an eye on her today."

Ms. Jackson rose to leave. She turned back with a finger in the air. "Oh, one more thing. I called

Catherine's conservator and let him know that this was not the first or the second time she has walked away, and that this was more serious due to the time and distance. He gave permission to put a tracking bracelet on her ankle, so I'm having one delivered later today. When it comes would you see that it's put on and that she knows it's for her own safety and protection?"

Later that morning, Patsy ran into Catherine coming down the hall from her room. Patsy took her hand and led Catherine to the Activities Room for trivia. When it was over, Patsy took Catherine to the office and withdrew the security device from the newly delivered package. "Why did you leave in the middle of the night, Catherine? We were worried sick about you. You could have been hit by a car or attacked or any number of things."

"I just went for a walk."

"You ended up at the airport. Surely you didn't walk to the airport?"

"No, but I could have. The driver was very unpleasant. He yelled at me and made me miss my flight."

"Miss your flight? Oh, right, the flight to Spain. Well, we were all very worried. Next time you want to go out for a walk, I need you to talk to one of the caregivers and they'll go with you. Right now we're pretty concerned for your safety. I have a little anklet for you to wear that will help. It's important that you don't take it off." Patsy lifted Catherine's left foot to her lap and clasped the tracking device around her ankle. "Now, you're probably hungry. Would you like me to have the kitchen fix you something?"

"No, I'm not hungry. I had tea with the man at the airport."

CHAPTER 35
MAY

Pecan trees were blossoming. There was a trunk show of Easter bonnets in the library this morning. Several women were busy trying on the fancy decorated hats.

"I just don't look good in hats," sighed Olga, taking off a feathered purple bonnet.

"I think you look just fine," said Fannie. "I used to wear them all the time, before I was married. Peter didn't like hats. Said they cost too much, and just got in the way. He never was one for buying pretty things just because they were pretty. Unless, of course, they were for him."

Harry stood at the library door. He couldn't take his twinkling eyes off Alletta, and her coquettish behavior only made it delightfully more difficult. She put on a wide-brimmed hat and then held the brim and turned her head to wink at him.

Patsy was happy to see Harry's attention turned to someone other than her. *Harry and Alletta, a perfect match,* she thought. She rejoiced in whatever joy the two lovebirds brought each other.

Watching Catherine deteriorate over the last few months had been hard on Patsy. Day by day she was losing her battle with dementia, and it left Patsy bereaved in body and spirit. She had to get through this day and then she was off to Carmel for a well-deserved long weekend with Casey.

Later that afternoon Patsy set up an Easter project in the Activities Room. Spread out on the tables were lemon drops, peppermints, pastel-wrapped chocolate kisses, buckets of plastic eggs, and several Easter baskets loaded with green cellophane grass. "Put two pieces of hard candy and several chocolate kisses inside each egg," Patsy told the group who had gathered. "Then drop the egg in the baskets in the middle of the table. When all the baskets are filled, the staff will hide them and you can help the little ones find them on Sunday. Remember there will only be one golden egg to be found. It will have something special inside for one lucky family." Patsy had found the large golden egg in the storeroom tucked into a basket of last year's Easter decorations. It would hold a movie pass for one resident and all her guests along with a gift certificate for goodies.

Catherine sat silently watching as Olga, Beatrice and Fannie filled the eggs. Beatrice kept putting candies in her pocket and Olga would slap her on the hand. "Stop that Beatrice, those are for our party."

"I'll put them back if you put back all the ones

you've been taking," said Beatrice, twisting her head toward the offending shopping bag sitting at Olga's feet. Olga put her head down and said no more.

Patsy smiled, glad she had bought extra candy for just this purpose.

"These eggs are so pretty," said Beatrice as she put a purple egg into a basket. "What kind of chicken laid these eggs?"

"Beatrice, a chicken didn't lay these eggs. They were made special for the Easter Bunny to bring candy in for the children," explained Patsy.

"Oh," said Beatrice. "What kind of rabbit laid these eggs?"

Patsy tried again. "A machine made these eggs, Beatrice, and the Easter Bunny hides them."

"Oh right, the Easter Bunny. That big white rabbit. I had a rabbit once, a long time ago, when I was a little girl. He was house-trained to a litter box," said Beatrice.

"No, you didn't!" Olga exclaimed.

"I most certainly did," replied Beatrice.

"Well, a rabbit is an outside animal. It can't use a cat's box. So you're lying."

"Olga, you have no knowledge about rabbits. You wouldn't know if my rabbit could use a litter box. His name was Harvey and he was seven feet tall."

"You have no knowledge of what I have knowledge of, and now you're just being ridiculous. Everyone knows a rabbit can't be seven feet tall."

"He was in a movie, you know. He was quite famous. My mom told me he died from eating the cat's food one day while I was in school."

Patsy tilted her head as she took the bantering in, trying desperately to conceal a smile and her urge to laugh. "Olga, why don't you count how many eggs we have completed, and Beatrice, would you go over to the counter and get another package for us?"

Olga concentrated, but kept losing count and had to start over. Beatrice ripped open the package of eggs, scattering them all over the floor. "Oops. I guess I opened them the wrong way."

Patsy was counting the hours until Casey would pick her up after work. She thought about the sexy new lingerie she had bought. This was the first time they had been out of town together, and Carmel was such a romantic little town. They were going to fly. *Imagine that! Flying to Carmel.* Excited didn't begin to describe how she felt. She was pulled back to reality when Beatrice grumbled, "Patsy, aren't you going to help us pick up the eggs?"

A few minutes after four o'clock, Casey arrived at Balboa Shores, looking more handsome than ever. "Ready to go?" he asked, reaching down to pick up her bags.

"Oh yes, I'm more than ready," said Patsy.

The flight to Monterey took an hour and a half. "It seems like we just took off and we're landing already," said Patsy.

Casey patted her knee. "I'm glad it was a short flight. I'm ready for this vacation to begin."

Casey rented a red Miata convertible, loaded their suitcases into the trunk, and turned to Patsy. "I'm hungry. I know a great place close by where we can get dinner. Let's go eat and then we can put the top down and take the seventeen mile drive to Carmel."

"You're the tour guide this weekend. I don't know anything about this area," said Patsy.

Soon after, they were being seated at Tarpy's Roadhouse, an old stone winery that had turned its wine cellars into a series of dining rooms. Each room had low wooden beamed ceilings, connected by narrow winding hallways. Casey ordered escargot and this time Patsy wasn't squeamish at all. "How does a bottle of Cabernet sound to you?"

"I'm ready to unwind, so it sounds absolutely wonderful." Looking at the menu, Patsy chose lobster with drawn butter and Casey had the sirloin steak with garlic mashed potatoes and asparagus.

When Patsy picked up her knife and the spoon dangled from it, she thought she must have had too much wine. Casey laughed and told her the phenomena occurs because some restaurants use magnets at the bottom of their trash cans to keep silverware from accidentally being thrown away with the garbage, and consequently the silverware itself becomes magnetized. Relieved, Patsy relaxed and enjoyed the rest of the meal in the cozy restaurant.

Walking out after dinner, Patsy stopped at a fountain in the courtyard. "Look," she pointed, "there are coins in the water. Let's make a wish." Casey dug into his pocket and came out with two quarters. They turned around, closed their eyes, and tossed the coins over their shoulders into the water.

"What did you wish for?" asked Patsy.

Casey winked at her. "Wouldn't you like to know!"

They headed toward the car and, true to his word, Casey put the top down. "That was a wonderful dinner," said Patsy. "I especially liked the Mexican chocolate bread pudding."

"Yes, I noticed that you almost licked the plate," Casey teased.

Patsy smiled and then shivered. "I didn't realize there was such a temperature difference between Southern and Northern California." She reached behind her for her jacket and headscarf.

"It's still only April. The northern coast gets colder than down south. Maybe I should put the top back up?"

Patsy protested. "Oh, no. Let's leave it down. I'm warm as toast now. I'll just pretend it's summer."

"Even summer nights here can be chilly. We'll have to come back this summer and compare."

"When I was growing up in Kansas, summer nights were unbearably hot. Sometimes you would sweat all night. But we had fireflies to make up for it, and stars so bright you could almost reach out and touch them."

Casey gunned the engine. "We have stars here, too, and wait 'til you see the ocean in the moonlight. Pretty sure we have Kansas beat in that regard."

The moment Patsy caught sight of the ocean, she squealed with delight. "Oh Casey, it's beautiful. Look at how the moon glistens on the water. And I love the sound of the crashing waves."

"Look at that coastline," said Casey. "We don't have a rocky coast like that down south. The water crashing into the big rocks makes for more drama." Farther down the seventeen mile drive, the ocean view was replaced with a forest of calla lilies, cypress and eucalyptus trees. Magnificent homes lined the road on both sides. Casey stopped at the

Lone Cypress, and they got out and stood by the car to take in the view.

"Oh, it really is better than any of those postcards," said Patsy, as she looked at the solitary tree sitting on a rocky point with the moon high above it. "It's breathtaking."

"You're breathtaking," Casey responded as he wrapped his arms around her while they enjoyed the view. Patsy thought nothing could feel as much like heaven as this. Later that night, he proved her wrong.

On Saturday morning, they walked along the crowded main street of Carmel, going in and out of the shops. Casey saw a teal blue bikini in the Saks Fifth Avenue window and encouraged Patsy to try it on. "Sure, why not?" she said and disappeared into the store.

When she came out of the dressing room, she took Casey's breath away. "It looks spectacular on you," he said.

"I must say, I feel very sexy in this."

A huge smile on Casey's face let her know he approved. "Let's buy it."

"Don't you think it's a little cold for a bikini?"

"You look too stunning to leave it sitting on the shelf," he said. "Besides, we have to go to the famous Carmel beach."

Casey bought the swim suit and was proud of Patsy as she wore it that afternoon to the white sand beach. They rubbed sunscreen on each other, and discovered that it was warmer if they laid down flat on their beach towels. It wasn't long before Patsy pulled the towel around her and closed her eyes. Soon her eyelids felt as if anchors were pulling them down. Voices mixed together and drifted off into the soft sound of the waves. The next thing she knew, Casey was whispering in her ear. "I'm getting a little chilly. I think we should pack up and go back to the hotel and you can warm me up."

Little rest was had that afternoon. Casey stripped Patsy of the bikini slowly, one tie at a time. Their lovemaking was as passionate as butter sizzling in a hot skillet; after which they drifted off to sleep, their long tan limbs entwined.

That night Patsy and Casey headed to dinner at Fisherman's Wharf in Monterey. The wharf was lined with shops selling souvenirs, fresh fish, salt water taffy, cotton candy and ice cream, all mixed in with a number of seafood restaurants. In one of the souvenir shops, Patsy danced from one trinket to another, touching and admiring everything. She picked up a glass dolphin, shifting it from one hand to the other as she held it up to the light, turning it around to reflect rainbows all over the room. "It's so beautiful," she said, her eyes smiling.

"It's yours," Casey smiled as he took the dolphin from her and set it on the counter.

The young clerk rang it up. "That will be fifty dollars, sir."

Patsy gasped. "Fifty dollars! For that little thing?"

"It's crystal," replied the clerk. "See how it picks up the light?"

Casey looked at Patsy. "Beauty deserves beauty," he said, handing the clerk his credit card.

They ate dinner at a little restaurant with white table cloths and candle light. The waiter placed a red rose in front of Patsy. "My name is Michael and I will be your server this evening. Our specialty is ablonetta, which is squid prepared like abalone. It's exceptionally good."

Patsy put the rose to her nose and breathed in its fragrance. "That sounds lovely," she said. "Casey, what do you think?"

"I think it's always wise to go with the specialty of the house."

"Very good, sir. And would you like me to suggest a wine to accompany your dinner?"

"Why stop now? Go ahead and give us the full treatment," Casey said as he closed his menu.

After dinner they walked to the end of the wharf. Patsy stood quietly for a while, her elbows resting on the railing, listening to the lapping of the water and the sea lions as they barked a symphony on the breakwater further out in the bay.

"I don't think I've felt this relaxed in a long time," said Casey, putting his arm around Patsy.

Patsy smiled. "Me either. This trip has been so amazing, better than my wildest dreams. And I'm living it with you. It's like a gift from heaven."

Casey turned her around and kissed her. "Would you consider living with me?"

Patsy was so stunned that she stared at him, mouth wide open, before turning her eyes back to the sea lions.

Casey continued. "I've never felt as connected and comfortable with anyone as I am with you. I love you, Patsy. I love everything about you."

Patsy turned back to look at him. She had never seen him look so vulnerable, his eyes shining with happy tears. He leaned his head toward hers and whispered, "I'm not trying to rush you. I don't want to mess this up by pressuring you, so take your time." Patsy, still at a loss for words, nodded her head.

After returning to their hotel, Patsy needed some time to think. She grabbed a scarf and walked the few blocks to the beach. She strolled along the edge of the wet shoreline. The moon made the bits of shell sticking out from the sand shine like diamonds. *Bud, what should I do? I think I love Casey. But can I love you and him at the same time?* Seagulls busy pecking in the sand scurried away as she neared. The wind caught her headscarf and her hair blew unhampered behind her. She felt light and free, as if Bud were telling her everything was okay.

She would always love Bud, but it was time to move on. As the evening breeze touched her cheek, she realized she wanted to move on with Casey. *Yes*, she whispered softly to herself.

CHAPTER 36
JULY

Arriving at Balboa Shores the morning of July fourth, Patsy was immediately directed to the dining room. She entered and found Catherine making a fuss and the caregivers having little success in calming her down. Catherine's hair was disheveled and she was still in her nightgown. She was holding onto the breakfast table with both hands, her loud voice ringing out. "Leave me alone! Stop pulling on me."

"Patsy, thank goodness. We're trying to get Ms. Hughes to go back to her room and get dressed," said the young server.

"Well, since she's here now, it's probably best to let her eat her breakfast, don't you think? Why didn't anyone check on her this morning?"

"We're short staffed by two people, and we could only cover the residents who need help dressing."

Patsy turned her attention to Catherine. "Good morning, Catherine. It looks like you forgot to change from your night clothes before coming down to breakfast."

"I put on my slippers and robe. I always eat before getting dressed. But today this young lady is giving me a hard time. She's rude and I want her fired."

Patsy looked at the supposed offender with a sympathetic look, then pulled a chair up close to Catherine. "You used to be able to do that at home, but here you have always gotten dressed before coming to the dining room," explained Patsy.

"I don't know what you're talking about, and who are you anyway? I just want to eat my breakfast in peace. Maybe you can get these people to leave me alone."

"I'm sorry you're upset, Catherine. I'm your friend. Why don't you go ahead and eat and then I'll walk with you back to your room. We'll get you dressed and ready for the parade. We're all going to the Fourth of July parade in a few hours. Do you have anything red, white, or blue to wear?"

Seated nearby, Miss Millie, Beatrice and Olga pretended not to listen but were failing miserably. Miss Millie, eyes sparkling, asked if she could wear her pink feather robe and slippers to breakfast tomorrow morning. Beatrice started whimpering, "What's the matter? Why is Catherine mad? She's always mad at me, I don't know what I did."

Olga threw her napkin down with disgust and stood up. She looked each woman in the eye with contempt and stomped out.

Across the room, Alletta whispered to Harry. "I'm

glad I sat with you, dear, and not those horrid women. You're always dressed so neatly."

* * *

By ten o'clock most of the residents were on the bus. The kitchen staff had packed up the cooked hot dogs and condiments. Patsy hoped the jugs of lemonade had enough ice to keep cool until they served lunch. Several staff members had gone ahead to rope off a section of the park for the residents with red and blue streamers. Placards advertising *Balboa Shores: the perfect place for your loved one!* were placed strategically around the area so that passersby could easily see them. The residents were escorted to folding chairs or wheeled in their own chairs to a grand stand view of the parade.

While bands played, floats passed carrying prom queens and camellia queens. Military groups marched with flags waving. The staff was busily handing out cups of lemonade and plates of hot dogs. Patsy circulated with condiments. "Would you like ketchup, mustard, relish?" The atmosphere was a bit hectic, and the residents were having difficulty balancing the hot dog-laden paper plates on their laps while holding their lemonade at the same time, so Patsy stayed busy mopping off chairs, clothes, and chins.

After making yet another pass with the condiments, Patsy looked around for Catherine, hoping to catch her eating and having a good time. Patsy's eyes scanned the group, but she didn't see her. Patsy checked with each staff member, asking if they had seen Catherine, or if perhaps someone had helped her to the restroom. When no one could place when they had last seen Catherine, icy chills of panic began creeping up Patsy's spine.

Then she saw her. Tubas, trombones, and drums barely missed Catherine as she happily wandered through the middle of the parade, amid bands and in front of floats. Patsy ran to the side of the street, calling to her. Patsy tried to dart between band members and around cars, but Catherine was just out of reach. The noise was so loud that Patsy didn't think she could be heard. Quickly changing tactics, she frantically hailed a motorcycle cop to stop. He was quicker than Patsy and more aggressive, reaching Catherine in just a few seconds. The cop tried to get Catherine's attention but, this not working, he reached out for her. Catherine resisted by clawing and trying to kick him. Mid-kick, with one leg off the ground, she wobbled, lost her balance, and fell backwards to the ground.

Her head made a loud thud as it hit the asphalt. She did not move.

The officer radioed for help, and soon several police officers had surrounded Catherine while others routed the parade around them. An ambulance was called, and as the sirens announced its arrival, Patsy stood in disbelief just outside the circle of police, hoping to see or hear some sort of response from Catherine. Instead, she saw blood pooling near the back of Catherine's head.

She told the ambulance attendant Catherine's full name and asked where they were taking her. An unresponsive Catherine was loaded into the ambulance and taken to Sutton Memorial Hospital.

The residents of Balboa Shores were starting to get agitated and confused. "What's happening?" "Why is everyone crowding me?" "What happened to the parade?" Amid the general chaos, Delbert sat calmly eating his hot dog. Patsy first needed to calm the residents, get them home, and then get herself to the hospital.

* * *

Susan Jackson retrieved Catherine's advance directive before leaving for the hospital. She and

Patsy arrived at Sutton Memorial about the same time. The receptionist told them Catherine had not yet been admitted. She was still in emergency. Patsy had always hated hospitals. *Why do these places have to smell so bad? It's like a cocktail made from disinfectant, blood, and urine.* She addressed the gray-haired receptionist. "We're here to see Catherine Hughes. She was just brought in with a head injury." They were told to sit in the waiting room until someone came to give them more information.

The two women sat side by side. Susan grasped her navy Gucci bag tightly to her chest, her lips frozen in a tight line. Patsy tossed her backpack into the chair next to her, looked over, and realized she actually felt sorry for Susan. *She looks really unhappy. Who does she have to come home to at the end of the day? Who does she care for? Nobody, that's who.* Counting her blessings, Patsy thought *I'm lucky to have Casey. I have the love of a good man and I have the friendship and love of many of the residents. She has no one to lean on. Why have I always been so intimidated by her? I wouldn't change places with her for a yard of pump water, as Dad used to say.* Having little to say to each other, the two women remained silent, lost in their own thoughts.

An hour later, a doctor came out and walked up to them. "I'm Dr. Militzer. Are you Ms. Hughes' family?"

Susan stood to greet him. "No, I'm Susan Jackson. I'm the executive director of Balboa Shores. We are a home for memory impaired seniors."

"And this is ...?" asked the doctor, referring to Patsy.

"This is our head caregiver, Patsy Smith."

Patsy reached around Susan and extended her hand to the doctor. "How is Catherine?"

"I'm afraid Ms. Hughes was seriously injured by her fall. Our tests show that the impact to her head caused a large subdural hematoma. A blood vessel between her brain and her skull was torn, and blood from that vessel is putting pressure on her brain. If we don't operate to relieve the pressure, the chances that she will survive are slim. Unfortunately, any surgical intervention in a woman her age, and certainly any surgery involving the brain, carries risks of its own."

"She has an advance directive," said Susan, handing the document to him. "Is the operation considered a heroic measure?"

"Well, not the operation itself, but any measure to keep her breathing or to revive her during the operation would be considered heroic efforts. Miss Jackson, I'll need you to sign for the operation."

Susan looked at Patsy, who nodded her head. "We have to let them do it. It's her only chance," said Patsy.

"I suppose you're right," Susan replied tentatively. Her face looked concerned. "On the other hand, why put her through the ordeal of an operation just to prolong a life when she's becoming less cognizant every day?"

Patsy couldn't hide her shock. "It's not *a* life, it's *Catherine's* life. Who are you to make the call that it's not worth saving?"

Susan said, "I'm not making the call. She's not expected to live either way. But, I suppose if it became public that we didn't try everything we could to save her, it could reflect badly on the business."

Exasperated, Patsy sighed. *My god, and I was starting to feel sorry for her.*

"What do you suppose Ms. Hughes would choose if she were able to express her wishes?" asked the doctor.

"She would want to live," Patsy said with certainty.

"She's a stubborn..." Susan bit her tongue before saying *old broad.* "She's a stubborn one, all right." After a tense moment Susan said, "Where do I sign?"

After signing the papers, Susan turned to Patsy, who was sitting bent over, her hands covering her eyes. Her voice softened. "Patsy, you need to go back to work. I'll stay and wait."

Patsy looked up. "I want to stay."

Looking a bit relieved, Susan said, "One of us needs to get back to Balboa Shores. I suppose I can get someone to take your memory group today, or we'll cancel it." Standing up, she told Patsy to call her when there was any news about Catherine.

Sitting back, Patsy's eyes closed momentarily before she answered. "It could be a while. I'll call when I know something."

* * *

The clock seemed to crawl, each minute taking longer than the last. After several hours, Dr. Militzer returned to the waiting room. His grave face told the story. "Ms. Smith, I'm sorry, but Ms. Hughes didn't have enough strength to get through the procedure. I'm sorry to tell you she didn't make it."

Patsy felt a winter-like chill enter her body. She had to sit down. Tears began to well and the torrid sea she had been holding in for the last few hours finally poured out. *Catherine, gone? The grand dame of Balboa Shores no longer standing vigil for her lost love? No more of Catherine's biting retorts?*

She prayed godspeed for one of His more challenging children, wiped her eyes, and telephoned her boss.

Susan's response was as Patsy expected. "At least Catherine passed before she was completely unable to function and we didn't have to place her in the Alzheimer's Unit."

Yes, Patsy thought, *at least there's that.*

* * *

Back at Balboa Shores, word had spread that Catherine was in the hospital. Some knew about the accident and kept asking for more information. Susan refused to say anything more than Catherine was in surgery and the outcome was unknown at this time.

When Patsy entered the building, she was bombarded by resident's questions. When they saw her tear-stained face, they knew that there was no point in expecting Catherine to return. Each one took turns hugging Patsy.

"We know how much you loved her, and she was hard to love," said Miss Millie, wiping a tear from her own eye. "We all cared for her, even if she was a real pain in the you-know-what most of the time." Slowly they wandered away, each to their own paths.

Catherine was to be cremated and her ashes sent to a distant relative. There was no one to plan a memorial for Catherine, so Susan asked Patsy to do it. The residents would gather in the living room, and their monthly entertainer "Mr. Music" could play some Beethoven. The residents could say a few words about Catherine if they liked. The service would conclude with the traditional balloon ceremony in the rose garden.

On July 10, the day of the ceremony, the Great Room was full. Patsy was surprised that so many residents came to say goodbye to Catherine, as she had been far from the most popular resident. Patsy closed her eyes and listened to the strains of *Sonata Pathetique.*

It says something good about these dear people, Patsy thought, *that they honor life and the loss of it.*

CHAPTER 37
AUGUST

Several weeks after Catherine's death, Casey and Patsy made their promised return to Carmel for the weekend. They walked the beach hand in hand, warm sand making its way between their bare toes. Patsy stopped to pick up every shell peeking out of the sand, but seeing the damage caused by many feet, she returned most of them to the sea. She saved the few whole shells she had collected along with some small rocks that displayed a variety of lovely colors when wet. At night, after making love, they lay listening to the soft sounds of the waves and the piercing cry of seagulls.

One evening, Casey had arranged for dinner to be served on the beach. As they drew close, Patsy heard music drifting toward them as if it were dancing along the crest of the nearby waves. A young waiter in formal attire welcomed them to their table. They took their seats inside a circle of lanterns that threw a soft glow onto the lavish table setting.

"If it tastes as good as it smells, it will be heavenly," remarked Patsy as the aroma of grilled tri-tip wafted toward them. The waiter smiled and filled the tall fluted glasses with champagne.

Patsy sighed contentedly. "It looks like liquid gold," she said, lifting her glass to his.

Casey lifted his glass. "To us."

The crystal flutes made a soft tinkling sound as Patsy touched her glass to his. "To us. Now, let's eat!"

Patsy dipped a coconut-fried shrimp into the mango salsa and fed it to Casey. He licked his fingers. "Mmmmm. That's a good start to the meal." After a luscious green salad with bacon and feta cheese, the waiter returned with the main course.

"Tri-tip *and* lobster?" squealed Patsy. Rice seasoned with coconut milk, pineapple, and green onions, along with a very good pinot noir, accompanied the surf and turf. After Patsy thought she couldn't eat another bite, out came a flaming dessert – bananas foster. "Oh my, another first! It looks so good, but I'm stuffed. I don't think I have any more room," Patsy said, holding her hand in front of the dessert as if to shove it away.

Casey took her hand. "What happened to that hearty Kansas appetite you're always talking about?" He lifted a spoonful of the dessert to tempt her. "Here, take a small taste." Taking the caramelized bananas into her mouth, Patsy rolled her eyes and made what she hoped were appreciative noises.

Still holding her hand, Casey continued. "Close your eyes. I have one more surprise for you." Patsy dutifully obliged, and Casey took the ring box out of his front pocket and held it in front of her. Kissing her hand, he said, "All right, you can open them now." Patsy's lids fluttered open, and she gasped at the glistening one and a half carat diamond.

"Patsy Smith, will you do me the great honor of marrying me?"

With a smile on her face and tears welling up in her eyes, she jumped out of her chair and flung herself into Casey's lap, almost upsetting the last remaining scraps of food on the table. She wrapped her arms around him and looked him straight in the eye, saying, "Yes. Yes. YES!" She kissed him and then threw her head back and shouted, "I love you, Casey Howell, and I want the whole world to know it!"

"Then put on the damn ring, woman!" The waiter smiled and clapped his hands as he asked, "Is there anything else I can get for you two?" Laughing, Casey told him, "No, I think I have more than I can handle now."

CHAPTER 38
SEPTEMBER

With a wedding to plan and all the details that accompany one, Patsy wasn't thrilled at the need to deal with Beatrice's horde again. Patsy put in another call to Beatrice's children and requested a meeting. Beatrice's family had hired a therapist to meet with her each week, and it was his opinion that Beatrice was unlikely to show much progress at her age. He recommended that Beatrice work with a professional organizer to sort through papers and dispose of items on a weekly basis.

One morning after leaving Miss Millie's apartment, Patsy stopped to check on Beatrice. The room looked suspiciously neat and organized. When Patsy went to get a comb for Beatrice's hair, she discovered two bathroom drawers stuffed full of dinner rolls.

"Beatrice, what are all these rolls doing in your drawer?"

"Oh, isn't my rock collection beautiful?"

"Beatrice, these aren't rocks. They're not nearly as hard as rocks." *Not yet,* thought Patsy.

Beatrice took one and threw it in the shower. "See, they bounce! They're bouncing rocks."

Curiosity piqued, Patsy pulled open the bottom

drawer where she found at least thirty wrapped pats of butter. "And these? What are they doing here?"

"Those are for my skin. Why buy that other stuff when I can get the best moisturizer right in the dining room?"

Patsy shut the drawers and left to report this new problem to Ms. Jackson. *Maybe it's time to move Beatrice to the Alzheimer's Unit,* Patsy thought. Realizing that all this stress was only adding to the pressure of preparing for a wedding in less than two months, Patsy decided *let Susan deal with it.*

* * *

With just weeks to go until the wedding, Patsy sat at her desk at home under an open window. The late summer breeze drifted in, catching a lock of hair and blowing it across her eyes. She looked down at the blank page in front of her and nervously twisted the ring on her left hand.

I don't know what to write. Wedding vows were not taken lightly in Patsy's family. She thought about her parents and how devoted they had been to each other. She was certain they lived up to the vows of marriage, even when times got hard. She had kept her own vows to Bud, but they had only been married a short time and most of that time he had been deployed overseas. She had been so sure that she'd have Bud around to *love and cherish* forever, but life took its own turn on the both of them.

She looked around at the home she had shared with him. The old, well-used sofa where he would stretch out and watch football; the small dinette set where she served her first meal as a married woman. The double bed that was hardly big enough for the two of them, covered with a flowered bedspread and overflowing with pillows. She would be leaving these things behind sooner rather than later, but the memories would always be with her.

She wasn't the young girl who married her high school sweetheart anymore. She felt older now, more mature. She had eaten *escargot*, for God's sake. How Bud would tease her if he were here! *You can have snails everyday if you want. There are plenty of 'em out in the yard!* She smiled at the thought. A vision of Bud's smiling approval settled within her, and she felt at peace.

She thought about all she had experienced with Casey, the good and the bad, and how it had enriched her life. Yes, she had matured into a woman and she could picture a fantastic life with Casey. She picked up her pen and moved it quickly over the paper as she wrote her vows.

My dear Casey, my love, my life. I now know that I will be able to love you and trust you for eternity. I give you my whole being to blend with yours as we complete and support each other. We will share fun and tears together. Fight and forgive one another. Make love and babies together. I love you and will cherish you forever.

* * *

The wedding was set for November first, one day after Patsy's birthday and her favorite time of year. She teased Casey that he should be thankful she had made it so easy to remember their anniversary. Casey suggested that they hire a wedding planner since time was at a premium, but Patsy wanted to plan every detail herself.

Patsy's mother had planned her wedding to Bud while she finished up her senior year of high school. It had been a simple cake and punch affair with a reception line and little else. Although her second wedding would be small, it would be everything Patsy ever wanted. A vintage car to carry her to the chapel by the sea. Lilies and hydrangea galore. A lovely sit-down dinner at the Ocean Room at the nearby Weston Resort.

Before making the short guest list which would include just a few friends and family, Patsy had called Bud's parents to let them know that she was remarrying. They wished her all the happiness in the world. Casey's sister and her family would be there. She wanted to include the residents from Balboa Shores, since they had been her only real family for the past three years. Harry, of course, would be there as father of the groom.

When Patsy informed Susan Jackson of her engagement to Casey, Susan arched her eyebrows in surprise. "I'm certainly happy to hear it's the younger Mr. Howell you're marrying. That is correct, isn't it?"

"Of course," replied Patsy. Patsy then asked Susan what she thought about inviting the residents of Balboa Shores.

"I would advise against making it an open invitation to all residents," Susan said. "Most of them don't know the younger Mr. Howell and might suppose you were marrying Harry. I don't want to be the one responsible for calming the uproar that would create."

Patsy refrained from rolling her eyes. "There are a special few who are like family to me. Surely it would be acceptable to invite them."

"I don't think that would be a problem."

With Harry naturally on the invite list, Patsy had to decide whether to include Alletta. Harry and Alletta had become quite the item these past few months, but Patsy decided Alletta would be invited to the reception only. *Lord knows we don't need her thinking this is her own wedding to Harry,* she thought.

Patsy accepted the fact that Beatrice and Maisie now resided in the Alzheimer's Unit and were too unpredictable to attend. However, she did take aside Miss Millie, Delbert, Olga, and Fannie to tell them her good news and ask them to join her on her special day. She let them know that it was to be a very small wedding and she would need them to not mention it to the other residents. Patsy would arrange for them to take the short ride to the small chapel together. She felt confident that they would be able to sit quietly during the wedding, appreciating that the vows were both joyous and solemn. After the ceremony, they would have the choice to return to Balboa Shores instead of attending the dinner if they were tired.

CHAPTER 39
OCTOBER

The wedding was in seven days, and Patsy had her hands full. She still had to organize the Balboa Shores Halloween party, write up a schedule for staff to follow while she was away on her honeymoon, and pack up her cottage as she would be moving into Casey's house. He made sure she knew that it was not his house anymore, but their home, and she could feel free to put her own touches on anything she pleased. She thought the house beautiful and almost perfect – she had some little things she might want to add, small things, pictures, books, and keepsakes that would make it comfortable and homey.

It was hard keeping her mind on work today and not on the honeymoon. Casey and Patsy were going to spend their wedding night in the bridal suite at the Del Coronado Hotel, then fly to Kauai for seven days. They planned to sail, snorkel and taste all the delights of the tropical paradise.

She was planning the Halloween party to start at four o'clock and last until dinner time. She had secured several costumes and various props – false ears, tails, noses, glasses, hats, and wigs. The caregivers would help those who wanted to dress up and then escort them into the Activities Room for costume judging. Knowing that many of the residents grew up with old-fashioned traditions like bobbing for apples, Patsy had found a way to keep the custom alive with a more modern and senior-friendly touch. Holding their hands behind their backs, the residents would try to bite from a swaying string loaded up with marshmallows. The traditional pin-the-tail-on-the-donkey would be replaced with pin-the-nose-on-the-jack-o-lantern. Patsy smiled as she pictured a blindfolded Alletta groping several of the men before being redirected toward the jack-o-lantern.

Patsy imagined how adorable Miss Millie would look in the Little Bo Peep costume she wanted to wear. A couple of table games would be set up for those not able to maneuver around the room. She hoped Fannie would not get so excited that she put dice in her drinking cup and throw cider all over the Yahtzee table as she had done last year. A couple of residents got a smidge wet, but no harm was done.

The decorations in the dining room would be muted lights with cobwebs hanging in the entry way. Black cauldrons with witches' hands reaching out would adorn the tables. The residents would help make the witches' hands by inserting a candy corn at the tip of each finger in a clear plastic glove to resemble fingernails, then the glove would be filled with popcorn and closed with a black ribbon. Black widow spider rings would adorn the ring finger of each of the witches' hands. Dinner would be Cornish game hens and yams.

Patsy was almost sad that she would miss the party next week. She was sure it would be a success. But then, who could be sad with a wedding on the horizon? At the end of her last day of work before the wedding she was tired, but felt accomplished for crossing everything off her to-do list. A happy Patsy closed the doors to Balboa Shores for the last time as Miss Patsy Smith.

CHAPTER 40
NOVEMBER

A clear November sky framed the small chapel in a vignette of serenity and hope. Wearing a simple, elegant gown, Patsy waited to walk down the aisle to meet her future and marry her love. Casey had given her a diamond pendant as her wedding gift. She caressed it now as she reviewed the life which had brought her to this point.

She thought about her childhood in Kansas, and the loving parents she was privileged to have had. Her mom and dad had been there for her marriage to Bud. After the automobile accident that killed both of them, Bud had been her rock. When he died in Desert Storm, she didn't think she would survive – until she started working at Balboa Shores. Her job slowly but assuredly became her passion, and filled her with a new love for these older, fragile, wonderful human beings. They had become her family, each and every one of them. Casey had come into her life through them. How she wished every one of them could be here today!

A radiant Patsy, taking in the moment, paused at the entrance to the chapel. Harry, looking dapper as always, was seated in the front row. In the next row, Delbert, Olga, Miss Millie, and Fannie sat quietly beside Susan Jackson.

Patsy wished that Catherine and Sarah had lived to see this day, but she would not let a tinge of sadness overtake this special day. How she admired these men and women whose lives had endured greater pain than hers, and yet had somehow survived. They didn't give up. They made each day count. She wanted to do that, to make each day count for the rest of her life.

Would she stay on at Balboa Shores? Yes, at least until she and Casey decided to start a family. *Which, if Casey has his way,* she smiled to herself, *could be as soon as the honeymoon starts.* She glanced up to see Casey smiling, waiting for her.

She smoothed her skirt, raised her bouquet, and started down the aisle.

ABOUT THE AUTHOR

Peggy Penwell Marsh lives with her husband in Sacramento, California. She has two grown daughters with whom she is very close. This is her first and most likely only novel. When she retired, "write a novel" was one of the first things on her bucket list that she decided to tackle. *Balboa Shores* was inspired by her lively mother and her mother's family. She has written several unpublished children's stories. She occupies her time with anything and everything creative, and she endeavors to keep her mind and body challenged.